THE FIRES OF ETERNITY

Book 2

The Past

By

Edward Beeby

Published by New Generation Publishing in 2013

First Edition

www.newgeneration-publishing.com

 New Generation **Publishing**

CHAPTER ONE

"This world is young, for others are much older, but old, for others are even now being born, and doubtless to one of these we will go when this Earth dies."

Thus, Quita began. Not loud but his words carrying comfortably. Ilex could see no devices.

"We, as all others, are children of fate's music. We are infinitesimal chords in a composition of heavens. We observe the astral symphony and brim with wonder, with desire to know more of that celestial spectacle we see, and of this world on which we now humanly depend, describing as miracles when our sciences cannot explain.

Once, there were no stars. No sun, moon or Earth. Nothing existed but nothingness itself. Empty nothingness. Without time, light, darkness, coldness, warmth, life, death. How long it lasted, who will ever know? Then living music of Creation played, at the command of its composer.

The flowering of a star from non-being to being occupies a span of time none will ever visualize. In eternity, a billion years pass not as one. There is no time. Untold ages must pass before a trace may be born into the cosmic extravaganza out of the wings of inexistence and, if it does not abort, there must pass untold ages more before it may collect with another trace and so begin to form one more grain of the stardust from which this galaxy and all others, every existence, occasion and suggestion will forever be born throughout an epic inexhaustible.

Spirit of Earth made unknown passage, not the faintest entity in the eyes of the passing stars. Nativity lent physical form to the spirit that would be Earth as a cloud of new faintly shining appearance, turning and rolling, orbiting its sun, growing hotter, brightening, entering a process of cooling and the vapours surrounding it, compacting into a cauldron of spouting liquefied metals and rocks, cooling outer layers stiffening into clodding shell, thickening and firming in the way of the skin that forms on gravy as its grows cold but volcanic inner rages cracked the shell to ruins, molten torrents overflowed but hardening after flowing little distance, thuswise every upsurge adding to the thickness of the infant planet's caking crust but not more than skin to an apple. Unsound birth, of a dreadful world, its skies a pall of gaseous smoking steam, lit by lurid flares of volcanic vents and molten oceans, circling its sun but sunlight did not penetrate its shroud of the smoking steam."

Quita paused to live with the drama. When next he spoke, he was astonished.

"And yet, even then was a balance struck when the sun, acting upon the infant world's pliant body, broke off a piece to be its associate through time, its tale weaving moon.

The temperatures fell yet lower, for the hot skies to condense, fall as scalding rain but turned again to steam before it could touch the hotter Earth until the crust cooled sufficiently for the rain to land upon it, and the rain fell as a flood of heated water over the forging body of the new world."

Quita posed, perfectly still. A forefinger stabbed at the ceiling.

"Now," his voice trembled with emotion, "unseen and unannounced, was Asturia conceived of the hardening layers to be born as hope and example on this enduring, infernal first night!

Earth-Ocean deepened. A mighty fiery convulsion thrust a great rock-island out of the bed of Earth-Ocean

4

and up through its waters into darkness rent by flames, fierce hot winds and rains. Still it was a turbid world," mourned Quita, "its cloud unbroken, without light save from the fires of the rock island. But hope existed!" It came as a cheer. "From muddy spoils of the rock-island were washing into its coastal seas the sediment and the fountainhead of all Earth life that would be! A broth of molecules, inorganic but rich with future! First pages of Earth had been prepared and would be written! The blanket of cloud thinned, tore apart! Light stabbed across the skies! The sun lit up Earth! Earth-day had come! And Earth-night with its moon and legions of stars!"

The gnome was a diminutive Shakespearean player in full ranting melodrama. "Asturia!" The finger jabbed, jabbed, jabbed. "Earth's maiden land! A rock bare and lifeless! But fermentations in its waters engineered a first complex molecule on which life chemistry is based and that first unapparent reaction which would react upon itself as the founding will to be and initiator of a glorious springtime that would inundate Earth. Thus do all share the aquatic birthplace, ant, eagle, lion, forest, cod, humans, while the anonymous morsel that was mother and father of all remains known only to mystery." The melodramatic eyes on the melodramatic face widened with incredulity. "Did its own progeny rid them of it as superfluous?

The infant planet shuddered on through cataclysms of its young growing, wreathed in stifling gasses, Asturia an untenanted, watery rock. Auspicious sunlight charged the spirits of nature! Invigorated specks woke in the Asturian seas as living organisms and food for living organisms to eat! Without hesitation the purpose of life was more life! The living will spread throughout Earth-Ocean, gathering momentum and change, producing more capable offshoots. Lines would change and change again. Many would change within their own lifetimes. Successful organisms reproduced lavishly. The coastal waters of Asturia teemed with plants producing solar energy on which other life depends and interrelating communities, energy providers and consumers, organisms feeding on decay, reliant on each other, adapting to the other's peculiarities. And the song of Earth creation marched out of Asturia's seas!

Stranded on shore between tides, plant life grew thicker skins to help them retain the moisture that was their lifeblood till the tides returned to their rescue. Setting and following a pattern, nourishing sunlight infused stranded plants with inborn wilfulness to reach for the solar goodness as if freed from imprisoned longing and need. They crumpled at first but will supply means. They learned to grow roots that would seek out moisture beneath them and help them to stand. Keeping to watery trails, strong stemmed plants advanced into the hinterland, softening the way for pioneers breaking away from the rich life of the oceans, for such as lungfish and primitive amphibians, to begin the animal colonization of the land."

Quita's two fists straight jabbed.

"The sun had been the igniter, plants the fuse and exemplar. Now sun and plants combined to enrich the air, kindle Asturia into a powerhouse of dynamic intentions and upswarm of ecological ranges quickly filled. Denizens of water taught themselves to defeat loss of water and to turn to their advantage the land and its air. Tails and fins adopted appropriate forms. Squirming motions advanced into walking. Wormlike creatures writhing out of the sea found life styles as insects with signal benefits for all of Earth's methods of living. Asturia!" Quita's two fists battered each other.

6

"Earth's infant song of eager springtime! Earth's onset of its saga of life!"

Quita's fists pummelled an opponent only they could see, put up their guard, the face highly changeable.

"Earth-Ocean superabundant! Asturia quaked to explosions in Earth-Ocean hurling waters and fires across ocean and skies, thunderous waves striking ruinous blows, giving birth to new upheaval, new land, to new land after new land coalescing into the one, joined to Asturia by inconstant bridges. New land! New reason, new ambit for being!"

The gnome skipped his joy on the spot, crazy eyed, subsided into scholarly purpose rubbing his chin.

"The new greater land abided undisturbed by life. Asturia persevered through chaotic destruct-ions building mountains, crushing mountains, torrid and wintry ages, creatures escaping again to the sea, into a domain of benign and stable seasons and multifarious existences, rude children of nature fashioned by where and how they chose to live, learning for themselves what was best.

Mosses marked green the greater land, Asturia a domain of thronging diversity. Into the greater land, strong stemmed plants laid pioneer trails. Saurian reptilians overran Asturia. Winged reptiles flapped through Asturian skies, heralding the advent of birds. Meat eaters fed on pasturers. Pasturers gained protection in herds, grew swift, nimble, strong, dangerously armed, gained sanctuary in concealed, less approachable places. Tree dwellers learned to leap, glide and parachute for ready pursuit and escape. Small mammals lived and died furtively. Scavengers scoured for the dead of them all.

Ilex whispered in her ear. "Anybody seen to be standing in the way of what others see as progress gets the label 'dinosaur'."

"Quite a crass statement from suicidals. Whoops."

She had picked up Quita's affronted glare.

"A walk through Asturia," the offended eyes castigated the pair of them, "for such as ourselves must have been a walk through a garden of purgatory. Its reptiles lived to eat. Eating was labour life-long for giants. Hunting dinosaurs intent on attack were not easily dissuaded, driven by their stomachs against horns, spiked hides, bludgeoning tails. No less than for others," the eyes homed in with hard edges on Ilex, "must it have been a life of worry for an insignificant mammal creature, not as big as a mouse, living a life of precarious adventures devoted to cunning among high, densest leaves, probing for insects and larvae under the bark with long responsive fingers and tearing away the bark with its teeth, when avoiding the stomachs of the many who found it not difficult to catch and sweet to eat, but holding out by its cunning.

Pangs will trouble Earth from inception to quietus. Vegetation clothed the greater land, harbouring terrestrial first lives. Volcanic vibrations of Earth's inner core caused the greater land to agitate and rend, held together hitherto by fragile subterranean and outer crust links snapping one by one to forceful shudders. The greater land fractured into northland and southland drifting apart, entangling in warring flows of the ocean and rending into further fragments. Asturia remained anchored though attacked by tidal waves and downpouring ash of the greater land's dismemberment but its living summer did not falter. New lives took their places. Lizard-tailed birds furnished with teeth and with claws on their wings flew and climbed to persecute the small mammal creature greedily. But change had struck that was becoming too much for some. The dinosaurs were sickly, their swamps and waters drying, their forests expanding and growing too dense and they could not move easily among the close growing trees but their day was anyway done. They were succumbing to attacks of ultimate potential development and sterility.

The ash storms did not ease, powdering skies high and low until the sun at last lacked strength to play any part, its rays repulsed and distorted. Its influence fell away.

In the enveloping gloom, Asturia lost its bloom. Life was still being born. New lives were finding their places.

Through the dimness swept an invasion of ice and companion blizzards, and terminal loss of livelihood for all not sufficiently adaptable and shrewd. The erstwhile Lords of Asturia could only stand stupefied in glacial storms raging at cataclysmic speeds, transmuting into ice where they stood, or blundering blinded in search of sustenance as doomed as themselves, dying in mid-stride, before they could swallow the frozen leaf or flesh their mouths found. Their waters iced over, their swamps became their tombs, the frozen land their bitter bed of final rest. From Asturia they were gone.

When better climes returned to melt ice and snows, Asturia had been cleansed. Few of the emergent were as they had been before.

A new choral prelude to a new dramaturgy!" yelled and pranced Quita. "Mammals, warm-blooded offshoots of reptilian stock, now stepped forward to rule and fill voids. The returning sun welcomed the full Asturian dawn of true birds!

One for whom the epoch of winter had educated its wits was the insignificant mammal-creature of the high concealing leaves, without stature, prowess or value but its smallness had come to its rescue, enabled it to flee

9

into holes beneath the ground, eating beetles and worms, attacking mice and voles, tunnelling behind moles to seize them. Its bellicose rapacity caused its hands to develop thumbs, making them better for grasping.

The insignificant mammal-creature crept from its holes to its old world laid bare, its trees broken, thinly scattered, surrendered to grass. Its future returned it to its old leafy ways but to fewer trees and journeys between of high peril, open to hostile view, waylaid by sharp eyes poised in the sky or crouched in ambush or running fast, using every iota of its vulnerable cunning for it did not take long for hunters to be always alert for it as is the fox for the rabbit. Grassland dwellers evolved and multiplied in accordance with new provision. Carnivorous birds," the eyes pricked Ilex with wry amusement, "of too great a size to fly ever again, dogs, cats, bears cast new shadows of menace and all with a taste for the embattled insignificant mammal-creature as an opportune sweet meal. Its efforts to comply with and defy its new situations brought departures to the mammal-creature itself, thrust it into diversity, presenting it with cousins, the diet of them all included their forebear, culminating in an ape who swung itself through its trees by hand, bough to bough, eyesight quick, accurate judgement and sense of touch vital but it developed poor defences of teeth, claws and speed and if deprived it of its trees ventured endangered to the ground and reliant on sharp wits to save it from enemies, acquiring a bounding bipedal gait for better escape. Too often its flight was too slow. It learned from its mistakes. Adopted upright stance to gain better sighting and forewarning. Banded with others for the better security of the many eyes, ears and wits of teams. Confusing enemies by scattering. The value of the team was without equal! The value of the family! Society!

The kin of man were quick to choose their ways but, vacillating between his roots and capacity, man was much longer deciding." The eyes pin-pricked Ilex. "Some have yet to decide. Apes as we know them attained intelligence to ponder in small ways and interchange thoughts using expressions. Bipedal anthropoids, no longer using their hands to help them to walk and freed to be tools of the awakening brain, shambled abroad with a shuffling gait in their searching for food, retaining good ability to climb and scaling to vantage points from which to scan for food or danger, retiring to nightly nests in trees or high caves or protective outcrop of rock, when their grasslands proved miserly exploring ever further, ascending onto lines of adventures, experimenting with what else might be food, finding satisfaction in carcasses and bones, no matter how rotten, questing for and attacking to tear to pieces living game, no longer shambling but fleet-footed hunters in their own right working in their family teams, loping head to ground, eyes, nose and ears tracking, interactive vocally, quickening into all-out pursuit and onslaught, themselves at risk from fearsome killers and packs and resisting them savagely, adopting their methods, accumulating understandings, recognizing the worth of the horns and claws all about them taking up horns, wood, stones and bones to be weapons, turning themselves into conquerors to be with two reliable weapons at their command, the awakening brain and manipulative hands, valuable sounds would become speech, breeding with others, with older versions of themselves and with new, braving the perilous grasslands to ever more horizons of eyes and the mind, and from the miserly grasslands gathering riches, attaining first human smiles."

CHAPTER TWO

"Man on Earth's dawning! A sunrise of short-lived lives schooled by the problems of meeting his needs but dawning man was at peace with himself and with other men he encountered. All knew sufficiency of hostile struggle without aspiring for more.

I speak of Asturia!"

An aged newsboy shouted his headlines.

"Do not fail to remember!"

Two waving fists demanded his customer's obedience.

"In their world of the animal men were inconsequential. It was a world of primal necessities and threats at which their animal circumstances compelled them to direct their behaviour in the face of death ever watchful, their only strength one another. The dark watches of night huddled them together in sleep but awake to the darkness, for the sniffings, the soft foot to tell them death has come. Even in their short life spans, few would discover grey age. They had not the luxury of dreaming wishful dreams beyond the heartfelt wish of us all to remain alive through another night, another day, another moment, their animal intuitions conscripted to dealing with hunger and thirst, all manner of other animals, weather, happenings foreseen and unforeseen, fortuitous and not, learning to wonder and so implanting their animal beings with seeds of what was to come.

Lessons ingrained through those demanding times evolved into innate ingenuity at coping, ability to consider situations, make judgements and inferences. They thought out more and better tricks to keep themselves alive, taught themselves how to gain some controls, thereby securing first human moments to spare for human reflections. Their main thoughts were perforce spent on how best to survive but increasingly accompanied by interest in other aspects of their lives, in due course mulling over the curiosity that was life itself from its every new beginning to that unending sleep and decay at life's end. Came the logical questions. What am I? What is life? What is my life?

Logical intelligence hunted for its answers. Ever more purposeful observation of their world and its natural forces and processions of happenings brought to light an array of relationships and contrasts and substantial and insubstantial existences, giving rise to imaginative impressions of another, indiscernible world entwined with their own.

The new conscious deliberations were piece-meal, episodic but inspiring and throughout the emergent human world were sown a legion of beliefs in a spirit world not in this physical world and yet its bedrock and well-spring, and in a spiritual aspect to all weighty matters and events in all lives. Added to this, visionary investigations by early seekers of wisdom awakened them to their personal intellect and capacity for emotional feelings, convincing evidence that every man and woman possessed an immaterial element separable from the body, in other words another, unseen self, whose true home is that indiscernible world, from which all arrive and to which all return beyond death. Convictions became traditions. On that world of the spirits and those phantoms, man had begun to rely.

Diverse geographic regions comprised Asturia, each with its own climate and vegetation, and certain denizens unable to live elsewhere. Saurian reptilians imprinted fracturing lands. Human species ranged Asturia, black skinned, copper, paler, wearing hides and furs or nothing but their own body hair, from

13

feeding ground to feeding ground on a diet of what each day provided, garnering familiarity with where to find which food in best abundance at which times, with daily and seasonal movements of animals and inventing plots to outwit them, fighting aggressive contests with fearsome predators for their kills and in defence of their own kills, with daring cunning hunting mightiest beasts, their greatest joy such as an elephant, and they would sit down and eat the whole carcass and be able to rest for many days.

Their lives were geared to the seasonal movements of animals but a rhythm of life existed. Between the seasonal movements and the hunting came more sedentary time to sit and think and be creative.

A copper skinned tribe joined company with a great herd of bison and walked with it across the savannah as a sheep herder walks with his sheep. Stabs and throws of their spears of wood killed what beasts they wanted, eating their flesh, breaking bones and skulls to eat the marrow and brains, turning the hides into clothing. But such poor weaponry obliged them to approach a quarry closely, exposing themselves to risks and many of their own lives were lost. Where the bison lingered to graze, the Copperskins too would stay, constructing homes made from hides and grasses stretched over frames of wood and bones, lighting fires, each family its own, until the herd moved on.

Family ties and common needs bound the tribe together. Language, softly terse, gave the Copperskins the ability to share thoughts and feelings. They were a gentle, happy people. Their encampments often rang with happy laughter. Dancing in time with rocks struck rhythmically together and whistling tunes played on hollowed bones entertained them. They ornamented themselves with pierced teeth made into bangles and artistically arranged on their clothing.

Mystical bonds linked Copperskins and their world. They worshipped water, fire, the fires in the sky, ancestral skulls. Water and sun precious life givers to be respected and wary of. Either without the other could kill. Moon and stars occupied minds as spellbinding mysteries. Fire their guardian treasure, used judiciously. It warmed their limbs pleasurably, cooked their food and made it tastier, hardened the points of their spears, lit their nights, kept haunting unknowns and menacing beasts at bay. Such as lions and great bears were frequently met with. The Copperskin family would gather round the hearth to savour it, feed it meat. Meat was left on the hearth for the fire to take when it chose. Copperskin thoughts travelled beyond the here and now. They conversed with their dead as if they could hear them. Appraising the smoke rising into the sky, they concluded that the smoke was returning to its home. Once upon a time they left the dead on the trail, or if they were hungry proprietorially they ate them. Now the hearth was the altar, the last resting place of the dead in this life, dressed in dry vegetation, for the fire to eat and for the smoke to bear to its home as an act of enduring companionship to ensure the dead would not be lonely, leaving the skull and bones to be buried beneath stones and so safeguarded from animals, and there they would remain when the Copperskins moved on, to be uncovered and re-join the family and worshipped when they returned.

The short range crudity of his spear meant the Copperskin must be an expert tracker and hunter but he hunted into forests only when driven lean-ribbed, made anxious by the confinement and hosts of unseen unknowns. An insignificant mammal creature, his premier ancestor, took account of him worriedly. Incited by a bear's maiming claws, he improved his spear by tipping it with sharp pointed bone, wore bones as knives. Sharp edged handstones butchered meat, cut up hides, cut through wood, cut the site of pain for the pain to be released, by his butchery skills he was familiar with anatomy. Hammers and hatchets of stone bound to handles with dried intestines struck and cut with greater force.

In many ways, man will ever be inferior to other creatures. He has no prettiness of feathers, not the strength of a bull, neither the grace nor swiftness of the gazelle. He cannot swim under water like the fish nor soar in the air but creatures are mentally and physically rigidly set. They have specialized each in its own distinct way, and their adjustment to a new situation is slow, taking perhaps hundreds of generations, while by means of his brains and hands man may adapt himself at once by making use of many things which surround him. He divorced himself from his animal status when he learned how to take control.

The Copperskins came to a sparkling river running out of an endless forest. This was novel. They drank and watched the bison swim across. The Copperskins were not swimmers. The bison avoided the forest to be lost in the distance. Birds filled the air with chatter and sonorous calls. Geese grazed. Their nests lined the river edges holding clutch of eggs and young. Rushes were woven with smaller nests. Limitless fish swam the clear water. The Copperskins spread out along the river, made camp and availed themselves. Hunters braved the forest, returned laden, reported open spaces, prolific herds of eland and deer. In pursuit of a goose on the river, a man poled himself as he sat on a log.

Days cooled and shadows lengthened. In a calling cloud the geese flew away but fish remained, and grasses bore copious seeds which proved edible.

Staring down at the river lapping the bank, a woman

picked up a ball of soft clay and inspirationally fashioned it into a bowl. She held it down into the river, lifted it out and carried it filled with water to her home. Among branches of trees she saw reddening fruit beginning to show.

The Copperskins made a decision to over-winter. Snows entombed their homes, pained hands and faces but they were thickly swathed and provided throughout with fish and meat and wood for their fires, and the snows encrusting their homes acted like a blanket, provided pronounced protection. As days brightened and warmed, with sonorous cries the geese returned. The bison swam back across the river, and men ran with their spears to make kills as they landed. The bison returned the way they had come. The Copperskins set off alongside them again.

Thus, trailing the bison, the Copperskins returned to this favourable camping site year after year, and all around their homes along the river bank, from the refuse of the previous visits, a burgeoning plenty of seed-filled grasses and trees laden with apples grew and always more began to grow. Always the geese and the bison returned.

The Copperskins realized the convenience of food growing close to their homes. With every visit thereafter they placed seeds, edible roots and fruit bushes and saplings in the ground near their homes for the purpose, and thereby were planted man's first garden, enlarged and supplying more food year on year.

The Copperskins were won over. A fateful discussion was held. A surplus of food enabled them to choose to settle, break the habit of countless generations, not move on. Immediately they replaced plants of no value with plants which would feed them. Young geese were taken alive to be stored in pens instead of eaten straightaway. The Bison Copperskins had taken a lead. Man was putting his days in order.

Man is an animal and will ever be but whereas other animals conform to set characteristics, man is a paradox, capable of noblest self-sacrifice and vilest treachery. He is innovator and destroyer. He may set out to destroy what he builds. He may be a lover of beauty and beauty's arch foe. He may be overbearingly cocksure and in need of every available hand of reassurance.

Customarily, Copperskins knew an attitude of lightness and joy, neighbourly friendship, fidelity, sense of duty. They were egalitarian. They did not believe in a supreme spectral authority watching over them and controlling their lives. Nor did they know disharmony.

The Bison Copperskins set up comfortable home on the banks of the sparkling river, thankfully aware of how agreeable was their existence now, and of the benefits of husbanding thriftily all that provided them with all they could wish for. They had taken a long step forward. Their settlement gave them everything. It had become a pleasure that they did not have to move home any more. Their lives were in their own hands, their minds mature and cognitive and they far sightedly concerned themselves with the seasons and so were able to plan. A thoughtful man shortened the length of his spear, added an attachment to help him throw it. The spear thrower gave the throw much greater power, made the spear more penetrating and thus better able to wound or kill. The increase in the distance between hunter and hunted animal gave the hunter better safety. An idea was conceived by the same thoughtful man of tying bison sinew to a bent piece of branch, and thus the bow and arrow were brought into the world, the most important advance since the mastery of fire. With this weapon, a man could defend himself or hunt at long range, slay or disable an animal before it was aware that he was near, shoot the fast runner. As time went by the bow and arrow developed to achieve awesome hitting power. Copperskin hunters used it extensively.

Man's lines would flourish or not, through every future day as through past. As a line lengthened, some would be born not the same as their mothers. To be different from a parent is not rare. There are no set patterns of betterment. One man shoots his gun with accuracy while another on the other side of the hill strains to consider if any use can be made of a stone.

The Copperskins continued their sensible judgements. Although the river ran close by, they stored water as well as food in clay pots against need. They were able to eat more leisurely than of old. They had the leisure to experiment. They widened the river, dreaming up a ford, enabling homes along the other bank. The river an artery beyond price. As of old, they scoured the wide plains. They hunted with deference and the wiles of wolves into the forest deeper and deeper still, setting out along their river poling hollowed tree trunks and rafts, educating themselves in the river's ways and offerings, hiding in ambush, climbing trees to ambush prey as it passed underneath, establishing aerial ways with ropes of liana, driving small quarry into nets of liana and pit traps, summoning hogs by imitating their sounds and surrounding them, returning with all the meat they could carry and with captured animals captured to add to their stocks. Wild crops were selectively collected for their seeds. They tamed young wolves to assist them on the hunt and be watchguards. They arrived at the recognition that successful domestication and cultivation importantly required deliberate selection, the removal of weaklings, animals and crops, ensuring sounder breeding stock and seed. But success gave rise to population growth, over time meant decrease in soil fertility. But Copperskins were wise to the effect on plants of decay, nourished their gardens with waste, rotted flesh, fish. Fish were ever available, to be speared or netted or scooped out by means of a flat pot very slowly placed beneath them. Copperskins became swimmers from childhood. Their river the hub of their all and a place for pleasure. They cleansed themselves with ferns that made a soapy lather, their clothes and pots. Lamps of animal fat melted into grease lifted darkness from homes and paths between. They pampered faces and bodies with oils from plants, bedecked themselves with feathers, shells, stirred grease, oils and powdered earth into colourful mixtures to paint themselves distinguishingly, and their homes and possessions, with whatever came to mind, with images of bison, for bison had brought them here. They tested other tools, made better tools. They utilized the forest to construct strong homes of logs, and learnt to coat them with mud to resist all weather and not rot.

From an ancestral camp site rose a prospering horticultural town. Fences of sharp pales kept out even the most agile hunting cats. Food belonged to a common pool. The founding civilized arts were happening, spinning, weaving, pottery; women gathered wild rice in a marsh and flailed it into baskets; grains and seeds were crushed between a flat stone of hard rock and a grinding stone, moistened and made into bread. Outside the towns, enclosed fruit groves and gardens were guarded by wolf dogs and children against wild pilferers, and in stockaded meadows favourite livestock were kept for their eggs, meat and milk, feathers and skins and to breed more, and there was always the river to be harvested, and the returning bison and geese, with prudence. It was never wise to take all.

Man, the inferior in many ways of other animals, was acquiring jurisdiction over them all.

The days of the Bison Copperskins were filled with need for nothing. They lived without a chief by collective decisions under ancestral guidance. For their want for nothing now, they were beholden to those who had made their final camp here, and deliberations turned to them. What would they have done? Many Copperskins now lived to grow older than their forebears and be founts of information and tellers of stories that would charm and advise their eager listeners. Homes, trees, rocks were lavish with carvings of ancestral heads. Transforming bowls used for grinding, a woodcarver added to their music the pulsing hollow booms and gentler pow-pows of drums.

In the jungle heart of the forest was discovered the perennial spring source of the river. They were now more than ever at one with their home and the pacific wealth of their lives. There were no conceited minds. Nor did death burden them. Their hearts were warm with the true joy of true peace."

Ilex barely glanced at the copper skinned hand resting on his leg, sat briskly to attention as the gnome's shooting glare brought him back.

"Copperskins were toiling but smiling. Men hunted and fished, provided the hard labour. Boys herded and assisted the men. Women and girls collected wood and were responsible for the upkeep of the gardens and household tasks. Marriage was in early puberty. Mate selected mate. Their marriage united both their families into the one. The newly married couple lived with the girl's family and worked on their behalf until the first pregnancy. The couple thereafter established a home and living of their own on the periphery of the town. All the family were responsible for any among them

21

who were not self-reliant.

From their condition of plenty, Copperskin numbers by the sparkling river swelled by their own births and as other clans joined them. Numbers within any area must be limited by what the area has to give, and as it became increasingly difficult for every Copperskin to satisfy every need, new families dispersed to outlying locations. From that ancestral camp site, a verdant city unfolded.

Ages rode on time's infinitude of cycles. Across the fracturing lands, anthropoid ancestors of humankind diverged from common stock. Humankind diverged onwards on disparate journeys through extremes of fluctuations of weather. Enduring winters, parching heat compelled men and creatures to look for new homes in all directions. In the wake of migrations, men and creatures alike remodelled themselves to conform to pitiless hotness, coldness, sands and snows, infested swamp, claustral jungle.

Throughout Asturia last vagrants were making their terminal camps. Black-skinned, copper, paler. Every group accepted sensible bounds to its territory. With every want catered for and room to spare, all lived without rivalry or quarrel. All marched with good hearts out of their savagery."

Quita's head shook a hundred woeful regrets.

"Fate decreed a new human strain with new ways of relating to the world and to other humans."

Stepping off his dais, Quita strutted several times from one end of the stage to the other, frowning, confused and disappointed at his audience, mounted his platform, expressionless.

"Emerging man left his parlous frailness behind and dwelt securely. Pale skinned settlers wanted more, divided into affluent and less, affluence degraded into rapacity, rapacity struck its blows. Affluent paleskins avouching ascendancy seized fields of poorer and made themselves into an elite class of overlords, the poor their lackeys. Surpluses belonged not to any common pool. The elite commanded, their lackeys obeyed, harangued by misconducting priests into believing in their own lowly status.

By bribery and intimidation, a Paleskin overlord supported by henchmen seized control over neighbouring overlords and declared himself their king. His intemperate lust was power. He seized into his power every man, woman and child. He declared ownership of all the land to be his but shared among elite attendants on condition of rendering loyal service and dues. All such dues could only come from the labours of lackeys. It was not enough. His power was not enough. The king's mind grew fretful. Lackeys were formed into this Earth's first army. Now the servile too would be takers of land.

Paleskin men approached the city by the sparkling river, the robber king with a smile at their head. At every turn, cultivation stretched as far as the eye could see, crops in rich red soils, pastures fed sleek beasts. The Paleskins concealed the short stabbing spears they carried. A happy celebration welcomed them. They smiled their pleasure. They wanted food. They were given food. When they had eaten, the robber king asked about the crops and beasts. His hosts showed him how best to reap and sow, how they could fertilize soil with dead fish to make crops grow better, how to tend animals, breed calves, use the milk. The spears stabbed. Even as they murdered them, bewildered Copperskins attempted to ask their slayers "Why do you take by force that which we would give you?" The slayers hewed many trails of many tears through the city. Survivors escaped into the forest, pursued by slayers but eluding them ever deeper and the interminable leaves and entangled shadows kept them secure.

They did not fight. Copperskins could not fight. Their hunting skills made them adept killers but their hearts could not bear enmity. They could not shoot their arrows or stab their spears into another.

The robber king understood this. His emissaries entered the forest calling pleas for an end to misunderstandings and for a treaty to lay down rules which would settle differences.

One hundred fugitive Copperskins agreed to meet the Paleskin king in their city. They were dismayed by its bad condition but came in peace, unarmed, with cautious trust. The robber king was pleased they had come. They were feted, feasted. Funny clowns made them laugh. Children played with toys the pale soldiers made for them. The Copperskins ate, played and laughed, trusted and believed. Spears stabbed into their backs, into the children, the babies. None escaped. Their city became the robber king's fort and summer palace.

In the forest's secret heart, the Copperskins were hundreds fewer but unassailable. Near the copious perennial spring source of the river they built a new, secret village reached only by secret trails, defended by ambush and pit traps of sharpened bamboo. But, shocked by their experiences, the Bison Copperskins, too, were being recast.

The Asturian sun awoke blindingly, lighting a cauldron. A day of hot suffering descended into night oppressively humid. The moon was full but subdued. Sweating stars held their breath. The sun breached the sultry night, red with wrath and for weeks to come. Crops and grasslands withered. Rainless days of tornadoes laid deepening seas of fiery dust, choked streams and rivers, the air. Waters ceased to flow. The sparkling river reduced to a trickle. Animals and birds disappeared but not their bones. Starving, exhausted humans struggled with blistered hands to dig out roots, on blistered feet walked in every direction to leave their torments behind them, leaving their bones among the animal bones. A tongue of lightning struck a tortured apple tree. The tree burst into flames and the grass at its feet. The flames roared amok in fury, consumed dead pastures and cropfields, fanned by tornadoes charged into the city by the dead river at the edge of the forest. The robber king died as a torch of flames, his summer palace his pyre. The city was razed, his soldiery wiped out or scattered to the burning winds in search of new homes. Flames leapt the dead river as if taking wing, roared into the forest. In smoke, Copperskins assembled round the failing trickles of their perennial spring, appealing to their ancestors. Their ancestors did not respond. Their spring died beneath sparks and smoke from burning trees crashing down. Trees exploded on the edge of their village and gangs roamed in brutal panic in the burning breaths of pouncing flames, capturing victims to throw them into the fire for their screams to fly to whichever ancestors might hear them but in vain. It was as if every ancestor had died and the Copperskins ran in blind hysteria with blindness in their hearts, harried by flames exploding from tree to tree blistering their necks, racing the flames and each other, desperate to be not the last, desperate to not die, applauding when the flames caught another and paused to eat, fled their doomed forest onto the grassy plain of the bison now a desert waste, a virulent epidemic infecting the hearts of them all.

Rains began to fall lightly. Copperskin turned against Copperskin for the slowly spreading pools. Within days there was water for all, the river in small spate and in a miracle bringing fish but conflict sundered the Copperskins. Now their arrows flew. Family preyed upon family for water, the river, fish, geese, stock, land though there was enough of all for all but cupidity implanted to own best waters, best land, more waters, more land, more stock, slaves, more slaves, lust for power, more power, for more power over more. Families divided in ill-temper into rival gangs seeking to dominate, seeking out new places, their arrows imposing their authority, Copperskin authority over Copperskins, over who were not Copperskins. The Copperskin nation disintegrated. Arrow storms darkened the air as Copperskins fought Copperskins over the lands of the Paleskin robber king. The victors made slaves of hapless lackeys killed the old and who else could not work. Asturia the bountiful land debased into a weeping land as Copperskin spiritual perversions swept into its every human inhabited tract. Rape fused Copperskin blood with Blackskin and Pale. Pure-bred Blackskin and Paleskin tribes would be no more, the rampant noxious sickness unending, hatred, artifice, bloodshed with trivial or no cause a daily and nightly normality, the poisons of cupidity, envy, malice, revenge! Cannibalism! Slaves and enemies, erstwhile families alike were eaten! Farmed! To be food! The land cried its anguish as the blood and pains soaked into its soils, hatreds and agonies flew on its winds as, fed by a paranoia that fed upon itself, one day to be a human congenital normalcy, even the lowliest Copperskin lived for the triumph of causing callous hurts, none were safe, not closest kith and kin, hunted down as amusement his ancestors, to amuse himself further by setting his dogs on them, cage them to be objects of derision and pets.

The Earth spun on, in the company of its moon circled on through the heavens, its raw humankind of the fractured lands walking their divergent, innocent paths while the unending madness blighted Asturia, Copperskin arrows manic.

Nor were the human species of the fractured lands destined to walk on untainted. All over this Earth, whoever they would be and wherever they would live, humans would obey their instincts and set out for a future bleared by its distance, hindered by obstacles and burdens, sooner or later arriving, thwarted, at the one, inevitable, most burdensome end. The most insurmountable obstacle of all. Themselves. Warped by unique weakness of ingrained zeal for strife, always they would walk self-deluded into the dead ends of self-destruction."

Ilex thought Quita was going to cry.

"Alone in all Creation," railed the gnome, a quivering finger stabbing high, "Earth humankind dreams of domination. He brings his gods into his quarrelsome contempt, gods of love and of peace, raising his sword self-hypnotized by self-righteousness against his gods' rivals, his belligerence such that not a friend, not a brother, a sister, a father, a mother is safe, not a daughter nor son!

"In Asturia was born a new splinter of change. In innermost dreams that stirred in their innermost hearts, they remembered.

CHAPTER THREE

The gnome surveyed his audience, their response to his rhetoric, displaying in his stance all the veins of exhibitionism his oratory had revealed.

What he saw seemed to gratify and he was strutting the stage boards again. The words tumbled out teeming with images as his mind leapt ahead to the next, delivered by a miniature Thespian with every elaborate play of features, pitch and passion of tone.

"A warlord here, a clan of cut-throats there, viewing with resurrecting conscience the envenomed landscape of weeping, shamed hearts and heads were permeated by one more tideway of the human progress until every faction, Copperskin and mixed blood alike, were moulded into the one, and with the one immutable remembrance. A sparkling river of pacific plenty.

Copperskin influence was all-pervasive, Copperskin blood omnipresent and realm by realm, territory by territory heart of stone turned shame into self-blame, into truce, trusted peace, trusted friendship throughout Asturia.

As Ilex tells us," Quita sang out, "in all the world such another sweet hour has not occurred to this day. Efforts towards it are denounced, quickly fail. Addiction to self and to the undoing of another sit easily upon their throne, passiveness a weakness to be taken advantage of, self-gratification a virtue. Men and women boast of their domineering of others who are made to live badly so they may live well, see their rightful destiny as rulers of all that is and will ever be, even beneath the beds of the seas. They seek domination of the Creation itself, relish its disharmony, boastful that they are the cause.

The wand of re-creation cast its charm, erased scars of mind and land, returned Asturia to a condition of bounteous tapestry, every thread in its place as a healthful part of the whole, ringed by its warm blue ocean.

Copperskins rebuilt their city by the sparkling river, and now they lived in a land of friends. The bison resurged.

Human progress will ever be a mosaic process of change, a system of flashes of clever ideas, long and short-lived, at the mercy of disruptions. Uniformity of human experience is therefore impracticable. We are what we have. We accord to our present however long our present may last, enter new experience, overcome it entering change or it may be we who are overcome for we do not choose to or cannot change. We are testimony to whatever our circumstance. Flung missile gives way to arrow, arrow to gun, our legs and the load on our back move onto a horse, if it makes sense to do so. Can we feed and water the horse? Get it through our swamp? Will it breathe our frosty thin air? Bodies and minds acclimatize to make use of whatever their surrounds, or are unable to react and thereby lose their way. Hence all over this Earth in their various places are the various races of men. So with Asturia.

Mutual forbearance and goodwill filled the lives of Asturians with satiety. Their lands provided dissimilar conditions which made them again into variant tribes but unlikeness counting as nothing. All men and women were equals as brothers and sisters beneath Asturian skies. Music was enjoyed, played on what could be made from what was at hand. Of his own accord, a Copperskin sage travelled lands and rivers teaching a language to be common to all, spoken and written, his wife at his side. Delighted approval met him. Volunteers flocked to be his aides. Clerics were thereupon asked to record Asturia's story, remembered and henceforward, in proper sequence for future generations to call on.

Our early manuscripts," Quita sang high, "tell of joys of wayfarers through a land resounding to life's uttermost song, a carnival of Creation echoing to the sounds and quiet ways of each to its own. Everywhere, within the dust, beneath the ground, under stones, a thread in the tapestry made it home and died.

Yes! Death resided too! Death stalked the idyll! But hawk and tiger are born with the right to feed and feed their young from a table of plenty. And how," the gnome's eyes inveigled, "can any live if none die? But psychic disharmonies did not plague the concord. Asturians, Earth's illuminated humans, had grown out of their fell past. It has been ascribed to the present being served by the past. As heredity passes down through the bloodline, so their fall into the evil of ego was stamped on their inherited intuition. They had set aside forever their spears and arrows of war.

Such was the aura of amity, authority was deemed not necessary, though women and men were appointed in each district to sit in judgement over minor uncertainties. The dissimilar peoples of Asturia in their dissimilar homelands with their dissimilar ways," Quita's hands and voice rubbed together, "were a harmonized one, imbibing their wonderful land. A wonderful tranquillity fell over Asturia of spiritual content."

An abrupt halt to the flow and indifferent wave told the audience he wanted them out.

"I can swallow some of it." Ilex leaned against the dog pen blearily and irritably.

"Oh? Which some?"

People overheard, stopped to listen.

He blew his cheeks out.

"Which some can you not?"

"It all sounds nice and neat and with a nice happy tea party ending but it is all too airy-fairy. He talks as if they were one big happy bunch of lifelong, back scratching pacifists, and they were nothing of the sort. They could not afford to be. They had too much to put up with."

"You were there?"

"'Dawning man was at peace with himself. Cooperation reigned.' Of course it did within the group, because they either had to share out the work and responsibilities or starve and go under. Living in large families lightens everybody's load, and there has always been better safety in numbers and so yes, some of them might well have found some peace but only up to a point."

"Which is?"

"Which is that finer feelings they could not afford. The only real peace they could have had any time for was a full belly. If they came across a good feeding area they had to stand their ground if others came along or be pushed out into areas where there was less. The strongest get the most. Remember your stag. The weakest get the least. So none of them could afford the luxury of wasting their time being mild mannered doves if it meant being pushed around. I am not saying their lives were nothing but a non-stop unmerry-go-round but on their own, as solitary individuals, none of them would have lasted five minutes. The only way to get through was by sticking together with disciplined teamwork, which meant abiding by rules with everybody knowing their place. The head man made sure of that. He was like your stag, lord and master of females and youngsters plus a few secondary males, sons and uncles and so on, who he kept in their place.

31

As soon as a daughter seemed ripe enough, he mated with her. When the sons grew up and he felt they were a threat to his leadership or went after his females, he beat them up and kicked them out until the day came along when he was too old to keep it up and a son beat him up instead and took his place, and mated with his own mother if she took his fancy."

"You sound very sure. How do you know?"

"I know because it is normal with social animals. If any group of anything is going to hold out, individual feelings have to take second place and, turn it around, the best way for every individual to be served is by the group working well as a whole. Rule breaking rocks stability, breaks up the team."

Her eyes brows arched quizzically. He pushed himself upright in confrontation.

"When newcomers came along with slicker ways of doing things, they would have had to fight all the harder to keep going, go and look for food somewhere else. When farming came along, hunting grounds were denuded and everything and everybody else squeezed more and more into less and less, and that would have been sparks for fighting. It always has been."

"That does not make any of them warlike. Yes, what you are saying does apply to most groups, to gorillas. Are they not peaceable and close to us?"

"They are when they are left alone, but they also have their rules that serve them best. Chimpanzees hunt other chimpanzees."

"All chimpanzees hunt other chimpanzees?"

"Of course not! But they are not even subhumans!"

"Nor is a lion but is a lion forever at war?"

"No! But they have a pride leader keeping them in order, and a thing about territory and neighbouring prides muscling in. They spend a lot of their time on the lookout for war."

"They are equipped to fight, and keep their eyes open for trouble but that does not make them naturally disposed to making war. Why should they wish to risk being injured, killed, any more than every animal they hunt? My story of the stag was only half its story. Sexual cravings excite it, and it run at full speed from lions and wolves but otherwise, generally, its life is composed. It is surrounded by food, and knows where and what it can eat the year round, and nor did prehistoric aboriginals spend every day worriedly wondering how they might fulfil their needs. They had learnt long before. You are basing your arguments on apes but the potential for apes to be flexible and adapt, learn new ways is very limited. The gorilla on the forest floor cannot pack its bags and go and live with its cousin the baboon on the dry desert hill. And of course! Everything protects its feeding space. A robin does not sing to entertain itself or anything else; it is telling other robins "this space is mine." It is one more part of the natural order, as is leadership, without which anarchy would always prevail."

"That is what I have been saying." He thought it was.

"Have you? And that the natural order included a violent disposition among early humans? You are confusing keeping one's eyes open for a threat with being on the lookout for every excuse to set off on the warpath. The gorilla is equable. Faced with what it sees as a threat, it will hoot and drum on its chest but largely it is a display of bluff. A charge at a man will nearly always stop if the man holds his ground. Among tribes that understand gorillas, it is a disgrace to be bitten by a gorilla since only a coward is likely to be attacked but there must always have been aberrant gorillas, of course, as with men, but so why would 'dawning man', exposed day and night to an array of perils, spend any

33

of his time thinking it not enough and wishing he could go to war, unless crazed? What they had might not have been one long violin concerto but it was a peace. Compared with what has happened down the human ages since, it was that bed of roses although, of course, all roses have some thorns."

"A logical woman. Can there be anything worse?"

His eyes patrolled her copper coloured face, arms and hands.

"From harbours all around their coast, Asturians fished the inshore, with improving craft the open seas, and ventured out into the great oceans and into many adventures, making contacts, establishing ties."

A stick appeared in Quita's hand. He flourished it, tapped a map on the wall behind him.

"With stable, structured societies here and here."

The big islands in the misshapen Pacific and Atlantic.

Ilex sat up.

The stick rebounded onto the island in the Pacific.

"With Tamalfua, Asturian influence gained small footing. Tamalfuan society was an association of extended families united under a hereditary queen, never a king. Tamalfuans were likeable, naked, impromptu singers, free of cares in an indolent way. Their god was their ocean. They fared with little stress in villages of rough homes of earth, on the generosity of their sea and abundant fruit, sheep and pigs gave them milk and meat. They took enjoyment from their sea, making forays on sailing rafts," the stick rapped brisk tattoos on islands and atolls dotting the blue, "raiding for women and for the laughter to be had from seeing people fleeing from them, and to explore their god-ocean, all they able to reach. Year after year, some did not return home. Marooned made new homes.

Rapport between Tamalfuan and Asturian developed, Tamalfuans admiring Asturian sincerity though finding it dreary, while for Asturians their roguish outlook was entertaining. Whenever the pirates berthed at Asturia, the welcome was never misplaced."

The stick thwacked the Atlantic.

"With Atlantis, it was another matter!"

Ilex tugged an ear. He had to be dreaming.

"Then you are dreaming me."

He looked harder than ever before at the close shocking beauty. He had to be.

"A land of water and uplands suitable only for goats. Atlanteans were unavoidably a people of the water. They were of homogenous stock of homogenous blood but sundered into warrior societies prone to mischief, of defended villages at river mouths and where rivers were wide and on lakes, the footings wooden platforms supported by piles driven into the beds. Never more than a single bridge joined village to shore. Such was the level of distrust, with cause. In the event of a raid, villagers sheltered behind their spiked fences, removing a section of their bridge. All of Atlantis pursued necessarily a fishing economy, with bamboo harpoons and nets from flat bottomed craft, and from shallows and banks. They voyaged in boastful fashion when times allowed, on resplendent galleys across the many lakes and from lake to lake and along the many rivers. On the prows of their galleys was carved the only god of Atlantis, a fiendish human-fish. Deceased were consigned to the waters to be their god's gift and sustenance.

The proneness to mischief was with all men and women, even young ones, of Atlantis but when Asturians landed with cloths, pearls, pots and tools as gifts, the local inhabitants were not unfriendly, and brought them fish as barter.

Innately, all of us are what we are. It needed no more than the initial widening of their horizons by that first visit to motivate Atlantis into action. The overwhelming abiding interest of Atlantis hereafter would always be trade. Aboard their galleys, Atlantean merchant warriors took to the ocean as if born to it, surpassing Asturians as sailors and navigators, and on discovering better timber, in ship design.

Fully fledged trade was established. Quayside markets served both peoples. Soon enterprising merchants of Atlantis were voyaging through all the oceans rowing three tiered galleys and in ships under sail on expeditions searching for trade, landing on shores that might give them advantage, ransacking sea and river beds for oysters and their pearls. If a shore were occupied, it was in their blood to fight to take it if they judged they could win it. More Atlanteans were lost in clashes with alien natives than to ocean waves but their colonies multiplied as trading posts and victualing stations from where to explore more lands and more seas for more markets. Asturians trading translucent green crystals guided merchants of Atlantis to mountains of crystal, walls of emerald, to sites of copper, gold. In its native condition, copper can be hammered and pressed without breaking. Truculent warrior society of Atlantis became ruthless enterprising mercantile society armed with metal weapons. Competing merchant trains crossed all of Asturia. Traders vied side by side. Prolific farmlands perpetually amazed them. There could never be anything like it at their water riven homeland. Asturians everywhere were happy to provide them with what they desired or were lacking. Their personal ornaments became of gold and thin leaves of copper that shone like the sun, and unflawed emeralds that flashed with green fires when they moved. Traders from Asturia seldom called upon Atlantis further than its wharves, limited by its nature, but were treated with civility and all was correctly done.

Asturia. No settlement defended by palisade. Its diverse peoples mingling freely. When a day was done they might gather by their fires to listen to minstrels, dance and sing. Many settlements aggregated into conurbations but the city by the sparkling river would forever beat as every Asturian's heart.

Tools of harder bronze replaced copper. Plough shares of bronze replaced wood, owing to the enterprise of merchants of Atlantis. No ocean waves however high or winter however long would remould Atlantean mercantile zeal. Atlanteans were not unfriendly but uncongenial aloofness made it not possible for outsiders to penetrate sociably their societies and homes. They were reachable only through commerce. The barrier remained in place, without antagonism, for three hundred years.

A power rose in Atlantis!" The oratory quavered up through the octaves, a finger frenetically jabbed at his listeners from the middle of Quita's nose. "A king named Aagon! Bringing new order and glaciation of the aloofness that had been the Atlantean way! For three hundred years," the quavering hectoring applauded, "merchants of Atlantis had docked from their trading expeditions to the old land with reports of its defenceless wealth and quiet order but there had been no consideration of taking advantage of the source of much profitable trade, for it could only be to their own loss."

The pixie eyes hooded, the voice churned like gravel, the finger wagged its street preacher's warnings.

"Aagon perceived Asturia with inordinate cupidity to gain it. Without discussion, quarrel or pretence, his legions waded onto Asturian sands with unflinching

37

cruelty. Steeped in ways of peace for so long, Asturians were victims of themselves, could only wait in dumb disbelief like cattle as the armed bands marched towards them and with axes and jeers of derision hacked them down. Many hundreds were slain," the eyes rounded. "Runaways fled with death at their heels into mountains, thickest forests and into swamps of bewildering complexities, and it entered into Atlantean folklore how whole regiments were lost and perished in hostile tracts with which Asturia was lavishly endowed.

Hundreds took refuge on a high mountain fastness, a steep sided peak. Their bows consigned to history, shocked into emotions long buried they sharpened long sticks for spears, took water and food and drove goats into their stronghold, piled boulders and stones at strategic points above the ways their persecutors would be forced to take to get to them. The approaches were few.

All across Asturia the invasion persisted, hunting and cornering without mercy and the hardships they were meeting in the hostile tracts turned the derisive soldiery into bestial butchers plumbing every utmost depth of barbarous depravity, severing limbs, skewering pregnant women on stakes through their stomachs, smallest girls abducted to be camp harlots, death the only escape. The refugees on the summit waited fearfully for the soldiers to come. Come they did.

Guided by dogs, an Atlantean horde arrived in due course with malevolent self- belief. Halting to gaze up at their prey at the rim of the makeshift fortress above them, they marched contemptuously on. Their assault ended in running flight from the stones and boulders raining and rolling down onto them. They reformed and resumed their attack. The end again was retreat, the missiles delivered with unexpected zeal proved too much.

At noon the next day, their missiles gone, wasted against a crafty foe launching fake assaults, the Asturians found themselves staring helplessly down as their enemies formed up for the end.

Under spell of death they waited. Implacably, tainting the very air about them with their cold hatred, the soldiers of Atlantis marched up unopposed. Downcast by this their doomsday, the Asturians huddled forlornly together, women, old and children ringed by their men holding their spear sticks. Frightened cries rang out as the soldiers breasted the summit, loud groans of wretchedness from loved ones knowing that loved ones would soon be no more and their distress drove some to the brink of the pit of madness. They did not understand. They did not want to fight. They were people of peace. They wanted only peace. They wished harm on none yet were about to be put to the axe because of it. A death so insupportable. So pointless. So wrong.

Strangely," Quita dropped his voice, "with their executioners streaming onto the summit, the wretched nausea faded and died. Some thought, if they thought at all, they had become deadened by their trauma. Whatever its reason, all had been taken over by a calmness, almost a kindliness towards their slayers. None were afraid. There was pity in the heart of every one of them for the soldiers.

It was not reciprocated! Yelling their hatred, their uncharitable foes charged! The heavens thundered! A roar as from the mightiest lion ever to stride this Earth shook the mountains, startled and halted attackers and victims alike. A second, a third and three black cylinders swept over their heads to hover above them and all eyes were cast high in an alliance of alarm. Amid windstorm and thunder two black cylinders

39

dropped onto the mountaintop. Doors opened, men ran out wearing clothes of gold. Running between soldiers and fugitives, without a word they faced the soldiers, swept them with beams of purple light and they fell to the ground. A number managed short flight down the mountain but hit by lightning salvoes from the third cylinder circling. None had escaped.

The strangers in gold turned their backs on the Atlantean dead. The refugees stood as stripped of life as the soldiers.

A red ball flew over the mountain, a fiery tail streaming behind it. A few saw it fleetingly before it disappeared upwards, climbing as if it would take its place among the stars and it was gone in a flicker. It flew so fast that those who had seen it doubted thought they had seen nothing at all. An eerie light settled over the mountain as the sun was intercepted by the moon."

The intonations quivered, the voice living in its homilies, the diminutive speaker an ardent player in the drama.

"Before any could utter bewilderment, a figure had appeared as if from nowhere, walking among them, wearing turquoise cloak and robes. He held up his hands. His smile encompassed the astonished assemblage. A woman who was blind returned his smile. The strange soldiers wearing gold added their smiles. Timorously, Asturians took their cue. And friendship, like a loving and beautiful wind, swooped upon that hostile mountain."

"I have had a bellyful!"

The gnome feigned mild amazement. Ilex jumped to his feet.

"Ilex, no! Do not allow your human part to take you from me!"

Her panicky cry whipped him blindly about.

"Come."

The gnome was stomping by. The whole room was on the move, sweeping him in his cloud of hot fury with it along passageways he was too heated to see, the gnome's bent back and crinkled grey head a fast step ahead until a marble wall blocked the way. The gnome touched it. It slid into the floor revealing a capacious mouth and throat of another, enormous cavern.

Already lit, the light expanded. It was Ilex in his tangle of rage who went in first, into a kind of huge vault that reminded him too much of a hangar, considerably larger than the last one he had been in and seeing through his hot clouds piles of scaffolding like giant Meccano models, three in all. The largest formed a framework at least four hundred metres long, two hundred plus high and egg shaped. The other two were half that size, like skeletal cigars. The back of a hand wiped at his forehead. He saw strips of black metal skin, windows.

Unidentifiable tools and equipment were strewn on every side. Nobody was working.

"Come."

He whirled about. The old goat was getting on his nerves. They all were. She was. Intent on bamboozling him. Succeeding. His mouth opened but the gnome shaped course back along the corridors leaving him following sullenly, resentful aspersions unchecked, clouds thicker than ever.

"Atlantis was gone from Asturia in a matter of hours," the gnome resumed as if nothing had happened, "a necessary number allowed to return home if they were able, to carry the word that Asturia was not for the taking.

Asturians, uneasily, offered their rescuers all that they had. Only their hospitality was taken by the fearsome strangers from the skies, not as victors but as friends. And mentors!"

41

For several seconds, Quita stood quietly, wilfully expressionless but analysing Ilex, the bitter workings of his benighted introspection. The lively little eyes flicked to Rashida, her face downheld.

"The strangers called themselves Venturians, disconcertingly understood the Asturian tongue, proved themselves knowledgeable of the deep Asturian past.

Taking charge from the outset, the man in turquoise conducted a revolutionary uplift in enlightenment beyond all and any imagination, in the arts of technology and science and their application for practical purposes. Almost in a single bound, Asturia leapt far into its future.

Tall and thin, thin faced beneath greying, thinning hair he was joined by a plump, fair haired woman, his wife, and a hump backed giant. His name was Theus, hers Alorna, the giant was Kardan. All three were in their middle years when they arrived. They took up residency in two farmsteads on the outskirts of the city by the sparkling river. Tireless in their friendship and involvement, speaking never loudly but wielding sense and undreamable depths of information and sound administrative skills, the length and breadth of Asturia would hold them in great and most grateful affection.

Asturia's crystal mountains pleased the Venturians since they employed the self- same crystal ubiquitously, as integral to the engines of their flying machines and in instruments of navigation and communication and mundane operations. Selected Asturian students in laboratories and workshops astonished themselves, harnessing crystal and light of day for generating power, producing heating, hot water, lighting, fabricating crystalline engines to power machinery, water craft and wheeled vehicles. Labours were completed in a fraction of the hours necessary before, with admonitions that many things were done better without haste: "Do not always look for quickest ways. Look for them in nature, and it will cost you your closeness and you will miss its messages, and it may be to your cost. Along this theme, there will be much about which you will be wise to think gravely before you proceed. The answer will lie in your heart. To your heart you must listen." The revolutionary wisdoms coalesced as a comprehensive normality, black cylinders descending the land over, their influence extending, crystal mountains providing.

Encouraged to not discard all old ways altogether, a grounding in anatomy and physical and mental well-being instilled an extension of the powers of the mind, a capacity to ward off sickness. Selected minds entered the neuro-sciences in depth, a selected initial few brought together, the concentration intense and prolonged, too much for some so perspiring their shoes filled with water but hour by hour, year by year, proficiency in intercourse between minds without aid of speech was instilled, as generations passed, inherent.

Kardan the giant worked at the forefront, behind and in the midst of it all, Alorna and Theus inspiring. The two were seldom seen apart unless perhaps when one were teaching. They would reside among their chosen people for forty years. When they died, wonderfully they passed away together in their bed, as they would have wished.

The exchanges were not entirely one way. The deep peacefulness of Asturians penetrated their tutors. Rain forests would turn into deserts and lands into seas and seas into lands and many mighty empires would rise and fall before the like would form in the eye of a mind of this planet called Earth again.

Ships ploughing the unpredictable seas remained of wood, simple to construct and durable, augmented by sails of crystal-metal, crystalline instruments engines, directed by compass, sun and stars and radio aids. Other assistance and advanced warning had now come to hand.

Before any Asturian crewed a black cylinder, pioneer pupils prepared the way, sailing a sedate dimension through the skies of Asturian and of the world. Few days would go by when airships were not airborne in some quarter of Earth, overflying animal herds in their millions, human cultures advancing or locked into their last or only season, thriving, living poorly, the violent, the cowed, the secretive, the proud. They made contact with some who had elected to live with snows and ice painting white the bitter north, with desperate numbers hanging on in erstwhile lands of plenty succumbing to smothering sands, descending to proffer assistance, transport them elsewhere, received without qualm as wizards or gods and passing into lore, filling many tales in many forms but tales that would never die. When those in trouble were the authors of their own sufferings, they were so advised and encouraged to learn from it. That all did not care to is the most peculiar human quirk of them all.

The population of Asturia, bolstered now by unions with teachers, revived to the levels before the invasion by Atlantis, and into an inter-dependant mosaic the equal of their land.

Intelligence dwells in many guises. It is not always apparent in which directions the talents of any lie. Many live unburdened by conscience. Many are bedevilled by a compassion they do not put to use, and act cruelly instead and find they enjoy it. Many may never discover themselves."

Quita shot a glare at Ilex.

"That inner riddle will only be solved if their efforts to find themselves are not restricted. Along the theme of individual flair and self-discovery, Asturian men and

44

women were unearthed to be the cream of theoretical intelligence, on many occasions to the amazement of themselves and those who knew them, directed into the realms of pure mathematics and all applications definite, possible, hopelessly far-fetched. Many, many impossibilities were overturned.

The cerebral powers of these who were the cream were dedicated not solely to theory but vitally linked with impossible accomplishments. Most spectacularly and satisfyingly, with others applying their intellect to events far beyond their shores, beyond the frontiers of their world.

The celestial heavens had ever been a lustrous adjunct of night. Divine powers attached to them. They had earned the gratitude of travellers. For lovers, there was no more romantic shelter.

Detachment transformed into intimate acquaintance, confirming suspicions never voiced that wherever their educators came from, it was nowhere on Earth.

In the study of the extra-terrestrial universe, Alorna came into her own, employing theoretical and observational techniques, mathematics, chemistry, physics. She dealt with celestial bodies, the spaces between, their relation to Earth. Introduction fed by enthusiasm made scientific study of the stars commonplace. Children made their own telescopes to tuck into their pockets. Visual and radio telescopes grew as common plants on heights. Its teaching qualified as essential.

In every subject, Asturians would mature enthusiastically to be the equal of their tutors, on occasions surpass them.

Asturians were flown into orbit, increasingly piloted themselves. Black cylinders continued arriving, and at home and in their craft it was a critical exercise to monitor the inbound out of the galactic depths, plot departures. An orbital watch on Earth was established, communicating with home on events and weather patterns, transmitting scenes of the world and near-space.

And yet, for all their powers now, when an Atlantean battle fleet was sighted and a new invasion evident, Asturians were at a loss, could only wait in dismay, hold to their dying peace very sadly.

It was Kardan, commanding a cylinder, who flew over the invasion fleet to pulverize Atlantis, who returned to loiter over the fleet, one at a time sinking twenty, broadcasting by voice the forcible suggestion that the captains turn their ships about.

By the time Atlantean captains berthed in shattered ports, Asturians had beaten them, labouring hard among the rubble.

For this they were chided but it fell on ears that could not hear. Even in the aftermath of their near-extermination, Asturian minds were closed to conflict. They were too far along their fated road, would not retrace their steps, could not.

CHAPTER FOUR

"One hundred black cylinders took delivery of their passengers and assembled one thousand miles high. As the hundredth vessel arrived, they accelerated into space in a loose V formation, Kardan in the leading craft in overall command. As they departed, Alorna and Theus passed away in their bed, wonderfully side by side.

Asturians had orbited and risked entry into space for short distances only but all were at their ease. Their taste for new learning unquenchable, enthralled by this latest adventure of body and mind their enthusiasm redoubled in the ships and at home where every instant and incident were being everywhere assiduously recorded.

Course was set for the moon. In their formation of a loose flock of geese, all knew where all others were and obstructions minimal. The pock marked sphere fixated every eye with inordinate focus. Lancing beams were eerily shadowless. The moon gave off no light of its own but reflected light from the sun. They observed no surface water. Their instruments detected none. The cylinders sank just a little into soft firmness as they landed among shattered stones and crater pits everywhere. Beneath a black sky, in special garb and colourless light they explored the Sea of Rains, seeing at first hand the sterile desolation of the most glorious object in their skies. Without trace of life or opportunity. Without air, without wind. Night temperatures lower than any place on Earth. In the day, heat of rocks in excess of boiling point. Silence, awe inspiring in its intensity. Their footmarks walked with footmarks of previous callers, and would add their ghostly lifemarks throughout the moon's forever.

The moon served to help them to view all other worlds through less romantic eyes but they were charged to take nothing for granted. "Romanticize. Be disappointed.
Encounter your dreams."

In total quietude, a hushed calm that was a living dream, they flew on and on, observed by a million glittering eyes in the blackness, caressed by feelers of an undying sun, liquid fires in their bellies a glow of intense joy and inquiry being sated and reborn. The calm was not complete. They flew through a typhoon of miniscule meteorites blasting through the nothingness to spatter the hulls, prompting fears that they would be punctured, torn open. They were excitable days of thrill and trepidation.

Came another, momentous cause to marvel. Aroused by the spectacle of their own blue planet shrinking behind them, by appreciation of the inordinate distances to the infinite billions of other celestial bodies that the glorious shroud of Earth-night, the stars, had proved to be, cognizant of mysteries moving between, living and travelling through an ever-widening veil of consciousness of a perpetuity enwrapping even the uncountable billions of years waltz of the universe, an eternity truly eternal, which could never cease to be, ruminations locked onto the transcendent question.

The beginning.

From nothing.

From nothing at all.

That all they were seeing and were part of and they themselves had been formed out of the unformed, born of the unborn, of the emptiness of total non-existence that time out of mind had always been until...

Mocked by the firmament they turned to their friends, to see them shaking their heads. "Perhaps it will never be known. Many will pursue the question of the Genesis. Most will abandon their search but we do not. Nor must you. But beware. We have been on this path for longer than we remember and can only advise you: look at life and to that which blesses and succours life. The agent of the Creator. Examine all that lives and does not live, and ask yourselves why. Compare yourselves with the rocks. Rocks were there before all living things of Earth but none are ever born of rock. A rock has no children. All of a stone is a stone. A fossil may lie within it. Look at fossil and stone. Ask yourselves: which part of me is me? The answer to Creation lies in the secret inmost depths of all that has ever lived. Yourself. The mite. The one blade of grass in the desert. Our engines are at work, and alive in their way, without soul, not alive. Be searching, find the Creator's agent. When you find, believe, as you believe that you yourselves undoubtedly are children of the Creator. His agents are his gods. In your ancient nativity you suspected it. We have among us his lesser gods. Some have been among you but you did not distinguish them as such. Find, believe, and you will awaken at the head of the path to the truth of existence. There you will find yourselves standing with us."

On and on through the interminable, incorporeal night ocean they thrust, exposed to hallucinations that were reality, investigating with eyes, minds, imaginations and instruments and the unstinting aid of their friends. All about them were stars, worlds and galaxies in vibrant health, dying, already dead, disintegrated, gone yet even the light of some that were gone beamed as of old, living lights without source, as if a lingering memory, such were the distances. They discovered imprints of vanished planets and moons, cosmic dust congealing, in distant years to rupture, hurl out gaseous atoms as seeds of new stars. They found a vast and ominous shadow, and slow streams of stars spiralling towards it, into it, vanishing into its non-existent black womb. Creation's end? Earth's end? Their own?

Undaunted, they asked: "What of other life?"

"Be patient," they were told.

It was not easy. They discovered worlds bearing evidence of life. Or, their friends on occasions reminded their eagerness, evidence of the possibility. They flew into tentative energy and light. Asturians would pay many visits to the ravaged twilight of Mars. Their friends maintained a colony there, staffing a tavern of rest and to observe the on-going decline. Mars had once abounded with insects and flora, supported by sub-surface waters, but it had drifted away from the sun. Now, its light and air failing, it was a wasteland never brighter than dusk falling into its last night.

The black shadow swallowing stars like a stomach had already caused disquiet. Now discussing the possibility that their Earth would go the way of Mars, they sped from its influence searching avidly for other planets with qualities to which they might be able to escape, and for those agents of the Creator, his gods, vowing to believe in whatever they found if they did.

Dynamic learners, 'if' was amended to 'when'. They had learned too much from their incredible friends to insult them by doubting them now. And they would work to ensure their children believed, and not through coercion."

Ilex sat tight lipped, restlessly irritated, taking stock of the attentiveness on every side, of Quita, who returned his look with a patronizing expression as if to a baby. Ilex puffed out his cheeks, wrested his face away. A sideways glance met a sideways view of green stars alive with stars of their own. His cheeks puffed out again.

"A young one awoke from her sleep. She left her bunk and tiptoed trying to not wake others to gaze out at the inkiness raining its stars in every direction save for that ebony stomach pool. She too was made unhappy by it. She picked up a telescope. Her eyes roamed among the constellations. But soon her eyes blurred. She turned towards her bed. As she turned, her eyes were arrested by a glimpse of faint glittering on the face of that ominous shadow stomach, as if yet more doomed stars were sailing into it. Her sleepy eyes remained with them. They were not, she decided after all, in danger from the shadow stomach but looked instead to be coming awake, and they were tiny, tiny stars not as far away as she had first thought.

Her bed was calling, sleeps opportuning but for a reason not known to her the girl hesitated. Although only aged seven, she found herself intrigued by a thought she could not bring into the open, becoming wakeful to solar winds she had been apprised of only that day, forceful streams of atomic particles, their source the sun. Particles were pouring out of the sun in all directions. There was something else. She did not know what. Alone and quietly, she contemplated the winds; the wider scope then went out of her bedroom to a panel of instruments for use by children and began to use them the way she had been taught. Before long, lights of the instruments were indicating and a screen was displaying intensifications of the winds coinciding with outbursts of prolonged and colossal hurricanes on the sun. A phenomenon continually repeated.

Undeclared thoughts were restive but the child paid attention maturely. Then her notice was drawn to a coating of x-rays inclosing the sun. She widened her attention to other, similar stars similarly enclosed and similarly disrupted by super-hurricanes.

An inkling took exciting root. Her examinations

were revealing patterns. This galaxy through which she was flying was loosely copied elsewhere. All contained their individual stars, aimless meteors, detritus of decomposition, starry gasses, nebulae glistening from self-illumination, to the little girl the prettiest sight of them all. But more importantly, every galaxy contained at least one solar system, each one arranged with its own symmetry.

The little girl drew back from it, as she had been taught to do, asked herself "So what?"

But her young intelligence fogged. She retired to her bed. But was unable to sleep. Again, as she had been taught, she induced her young mind to relax, grow calm. And, not quite asleep, in its condition of motionless activity her mind declared what she had seen. Patterns all centred on a sun.

As if cleansed of the prison of the womb by birth, the wax in her young mind dissipated. As unclogged, receptive and open to suggestion as a new-born baby, her mind engaged with flowers, trees, crops, harvests, all owing their happenings, yes, to water, but more than to water, to the sun. Beasts grazed sun-filled plant growth, beasts and plant growth gave people their essentials. Infant oak, corn and tulip alike looked to light even when buried, and when the light warmed pushed determinedly out of bulb and seed towards it, into the light and warmth of the sun. To begin again, perpetuate the cycle of their existence...

The little girl restrained her racing rationalities. It took a brave effort. Another thought occurred. She had listened to stories of how the light and warmth of the sun had helped Earth to be fertile. And when days and nights were cold, lacking the ways and protection of animals, people looked to their fires to remove the chill from their bones that would otherwise kill them, till there was no longer a need, when warmth came from elsewhere to help sustain them. From a giant fire. From the sun.

She saw it in resonant clarity.

"The sun is our Godstar! As the old ancients said! Our agent of the Creator!"

Shrill in her excitement, she rushed to wake her mother and father, startling her two brothers awake, to inform them as calmly as she could of her idea.

No! Of her certainty!

As her mother and father sleepily listened and heard, a red comet with a fiery tail bulleted out of the blackness and over the fleet to dive at the sun.

As if at a signal, Kardan died.

They were barely beyond the influence of Mars. Lights leapt at them out of the blackness. A globe of flames cast dancing lights and shadows over a planet of colours. The dancing colours expanded as the ships flew nearer. The outline being shaped was a world of ocean and islands, its diameter and that of its sun not greater than the north of these Americas. Its sun had balmy year-long effect. The fleet touched down on a flowery prairie. An encircling throng rushed laughing to greet them. Others whizzed over their heads strapped in light harness. They were escorted through an arcade of flowers to a garden of more flowers where the Venturian leaders were waiting, and laughing.

The planet Venturia was a world of many islands but only one people, under the light handed sway of a vivacious, red headed young couple, Calysos and Dintia, and their Counsellor, whose office was not easy. King and queen often seemed to harken to not a word. Both were slim, in many ways like siblings, though this was disproved, a lively duo given to pleasure though not to depravity, their lax and rollicking manner contagious. Their overriding concern was today. The past was the past. Wherever he went, Calysos carried a light toned marimba, his consort a lyre played with a bow. Although boisterous, both were capable of superlative tact and consolation in times of stress, and had been occupied when the fleet arrived. Only days before, a survey vessel had broken up in a battle against the gravitational pull of Saturn but the celebrations to mark the coming of the Asturians commanded.

The system of government was loose, the two rulers outwardly little more than figure heads. Enjoying themselves, infected by the two sovereigns, the guests were taken on frolicsome tours and everywhere, with Venturia recoiling from its disaster, the mood of the young couple won through.

The climate and island surfaces were of Earth but softer and without snows of winter. Crystals splashed hills with glowing shades." Quita stabbed his needle eyes deep into Ilex. "A paucity of land meant intimacy with wild nature but human homes were subterrestrial, beneath dressings of botanical parks. Adventures into the wilds were instigated and encouraged for the physical and mental exercise and as adversities to enhance psychological balance, nothing more deadly than a camera allowed, nor retribution against any creature unless it were suffering or carried disease or else mad. A laudable attitude." The needle eyes stabbed into Ilex. "Made possible by sound and stable human and non-human populations. And made possible," the eyes clawed, "by Venturian certainty that the human condition was granted them again and again, of which they had soundest proof.

Venturians were not able to explain it and did not try but Dintia and Calysos had been with them before and through spells of disaster. There had been several these last five years alone since the young monarchs had arrived. For longer than the archives recalled there had been bad occasions. The most distant past was sunlessly opaque. It was as if every Venturian had been woken from a sleep without dreams to a singular status, and a tradition of consequence designed to test them, make them walk with heads bowed in abject denial. Alorna and Theus had not been newcomers. Nor was this Counsellor Quita's first time among them. Nor had it been Kardan's. Nor were ordinary folk excluded from the reincarnation process. Each and every man, woman and child alive on Venturia today had been recorded as the self-same personalities before. Diaries, photographs, film and heirlooms were available as surplus witness.

Asturians were told: "You may accept it, or not, as you wish. There can be no guarantee but be undeterred, and who knows? Believe, and you may find a special place in the Creation for you. Accept the possibility, or not, as you wish.

As one, the Asturians frowned. "Between us there have been marriages, on Earth. How can you tell us that children of those marriages have been born before? For their parents, their union and parenthood must have been for the first time."

Challenge met with challenge. "Why?"

The visit lasted for six memorable, laughing years of sophisticated gadgetry and intellectual pursuit.

Subconsciously at first, Asturian minds compulsively meditated on the young monarchs. Dintia sparkling, bubbly, attentive, a story book princess and effulgent star to disperse ill wind, dark cloud, perfect embodiment of a feminine deity. Calysos demanding calculated study before transcendent qualities were to be found among the laughter lines.

The Asturians held back, on impulse wishing to believe but could the duo be a trick? False lures along a false trail?

It was in their sixth year when their considerat-ions approached a grave conclusion.

Dintia was a likely goddess and effective. Calysos an unlikely god but effective.

It was an hour of onerous accountability, their conclusion unproven and unsure but their minds remaining open and receptive, reliving the naive certitudes of the seven year old girl, and her example dissolving the disordered doubts like dew in a risen sun.

Dintia and Calysos were deities. Lesser gods. Minor agents of the Creator

The analysis progressed with clarity.

The partnership of Dintia and Calysos had been paralleled in the leadership of Alorna and Theus.

Alorna and Theus were deities. Lesser gods. Minor agents of the Creator.

Quita and Kardan were analogous, critically involved, but not the same. They were not gods."

"No, Ilex! No!"

He threw himself through a door, purblind, lost his way. Yelled at her to go away. Marble blocked his way. He did not know if this was the one, no keyhole, latch, bolt, bar, nothing, not knowing what he was looking for ended up kicking it, a Copperskin hand appearing, the marble opening.

The framework of girders took up over half of the vastness of the hangar, dwarfing him substantially, what reminded him of a railway carriage hooked to its underside. He paced out its length. Five hundred steps. Longer than a Zeppelin, he thought. If it had been an airship. He entered the carriage through a hole where a door had been to an office of electronics like the bridge of a ship, wall charts of an unrecognisable Earth, weather charts in folders; pushed buttons and twirled knobs on consoles he was able to make no sense of, pried behind television screens a millimetre thick, no wiring or evidence of wiring, bringing to mind some of the reported scientific developments of the Germans, the airship Hindenburg, reports of an Aryan colony in Paraguay, moved on only when prepared, through a door into a corridor to compartments with windows, berths, tables, seating, more televisions, a room kitted out as a galley, a door let him out into the framework, walkways, what could have been cargo holds, cells that held lifting gas, twin engine units very much more futuristic than the motor in Pegasus. Swung down into the 'hangar', walked about, seeing more of what he did not want to see, machinery, tools, electronic items he could not begin to guess at. In a drawer of a metal cupboard a ledger of what might have been plans and data of a black cylinder. Climbed metal steps into a carcass of a black cylinder. Eyes and mind passing over rows of panels and screens, doors opened to residues of what could have been living quarters, he sat on a soft sofa between soft armchairs and stared out through a round window at a sister hulk parked alongside, cursorily played the part of an inquisitive seven year old girl, found himself sitting in a cockpit, outwardly unmoved, inwardly choking with the certainty he did not want to accept, that these derelict piles had once been much, much more.

His feet took him to a sideroom, where he knew she would be. A library. She said nothing but opened and left open ledgers listing names, stores, requirements, a book containing a daily detailed record of a journey from Earth to the moon, another of a trip to Saturn, a narrow shave. Diaries, notes, photographs detailed homely events, children born in flight, the names they had been given, sometimes a reason why, one boy had spent his ninth birthday re-united with playmates on Mars. Into the night, she showed him films on a television screen of black cigar shapes lifting off; an airship rising from moorings with a cargo of waving hands; a red haired couple "Dintia, Calysos"; stunning shots of animal herds covering hundreds of miles of "what is now Africa"; she invaded his mindlessness with a Bantu migration into Africa out of South East Asia, "They are unknowingly returning home." He looked down on naked coal black aboriginals on the hunt with wooden spears, surrounding and killing a kangaroo; on a man and woman playing what looked like chess but on a round board; a donkey train crossing a fantastically curvy towered bridge spanning a gorge; a village built wholly of colourful stones. The most humbling were the views of the rotating planet.

His feet alone marched him with her the following morning in the cloud of bitter perplexities that would never leave him.

"Inter-marriages by now were commonplace," Quita picked up his theme as if having broken off to sip water, "voyages between Earth and Venturia regular and two way, until there would be few among both peoples who had not made the passage.

Asturian inclusion in adventures of discovery made them party to the study of Mars, landed them brashly on the furnace that was Mercury. From Mercury, their friends once thought they had chanced upon a moon of the sun, and pioneers had gone there, confident in the knowledge that the sun was their god and would welcome them. Craft and crews had melted without sign of their destination.

Great Jupiter held no attractions, a bloated gasbag of weather systems larger than Earth but Jupiter's attendant moons made for debate. Amalthea, too overwhelmed by its cardinal planet's brightness to be studied from Earth, reflected Jupiter's brilliance with a flamboyant aurora of restless sparkles. Io, in continuous eruption. Europa, a nugget of ice. Ganymede, yellow ice festooned with gasses. Callisto likewise, gasses less dense. Hestia, the sixth, not unlike Earth's moon, a deserted, dim, dead globe, winds with wintry teeth, there was nothing to which any hardiest, minutest life form might strive to cling and yet stone buildings stood in a township, doors and windows swinging and banging, wind damaged testimonials to a forbidding closed book.

Two more moons were of gas. The extreme four moved in retrograde direction as icy rocks sufficiently aloof from Jupiter to be under the gravitational pull of the sun. In their special garb, Asturians walked the outermost moon in pitch darkness heavy with feelings, with resentful, melancholic loneliness of no hope for anything more than this unyielding dark of a tomb. They were glad to leave it. By coincidence, or not, men on Earth would name that twelfth moon Hades.

The moons of Saturn were airless balls of ice, the one exception Titan with a half-breathable atmosphere of opaque orange clouds. Tentative plans were afoot to assess the feasibility of establishing a colony there.

Venturian exploration of space had been continuous for four thousand Earth-years. They had visited Earth from inception, in an educational watch on its progress. In the beginning, long distance research had been reliant on probes, fired in multiple salvoes, series after series. Probes remained in use, and probes of old were still in action, instruments pouring back data from cosmic extremes. On the twentieth anniversary of the initial Asturian touch down on Venturia, a probe was ready for launch from the Asturian homeland on Earth, assembled and prepared by Asturian scientists supervised by Quita.

On the morning of the launch came news that

Calysos and Dintia had disappeared, then the news that Quita, pre-eminent in their tutelage, had passed away in his study. Questions and dismay were granted no time. The guiding hand of the Counsellor had been lost but the probe leapt from its launching pad, cheered on, the sedateness of the tracking station broken by a yell and an Asturian scientist dashed out into the corridors waving a sheaf of papers. Etchings on the papers might have been scrawlings of a small, bored child but the message of their meaning sped like wildfire.

There were the forlorn remnants of flora and insects on Mars, the ghost settlement on Hestia. Now, on a planet sixteen million light years distant in the constellation of Aquila, activities caused not by weather or upheaval were being registered.

They were no longer alone!

An ancient probe, fired four thousand years before, had crashed onto the planet, instruments intact, and signals only now reaching home were reporting the impact and a presence of oxygen, movements of animal life. Actions of bees!"

Quita gave a jubilant skip that brought Ilex close to laughing for the first time in what felt like years.

"Creation at work! At sixteen light years, Aquila a neighbour!

Three special vessels were designed and put together, one in Asturia, the largest that would be known, equipped as towns and towns they would be, streets and homes of all the generations for as long as the odyssey would take. Unthinkable madness! Too many volunteers! Selections were made by drawing lots, half from Venturia, half from Asturia.

The vessels were twenty five years in the building but a week arrived when all three lifted into the air. They made rendezvous at Mars. Switching to vectored propulsion feeding off starlight, they set course for the bright star Altair, dominating the planet they sought. The enterprise would be monitored and chronicled night and day in the ships and in the enthralled home-worlds they were leaving behind.

Altair proved a canny guide, greater than their sun, double its temperature and ten times more luminous, a fainter star to either side, a lure among lures. Now it lured the three ships.

Before the first Earth-year had gone by, one ship veered off course, drove off into space without responding to signals and vanished from the screens.

After eighty years, a second seemed to vaporize.

Intrepidly, the third hastened on at a speed of twenty million miles every Earth-year through an unchanging cosmos pervaded with change. Only when at rest were crew members idle. They too remained the same and yet not, were born, gave birth, sired, mothered, were vital, grew feeble, passed on; journeying on through their centuries generating new frontiers in their minds as fertile intellect sowed its own seeds. In the lonesome isolation of the celestial firmament that was their lifelong prison, it was not difficult to gaze out wonderingly at such secretive beauty, for inventive empathy to wander unchecked, given free rein to caprice, to abstract delusions. To conjure up, rhapsodize of other things. For it is part of the human entity to delight in engendering dreams.

So was it real or imagined, another ship which flew across their bows, flew alongside them? A vague image which for a moment seemed to enter the hull of their own?

And were they totally foreign, the strangers in red who began walking among them with novel abilities fantastically superior to their own?

What was certain, no sooner had the phantom ship, the men and women in red appeared than they found their technologies improving more swiftly than they could keep up with, as if from selective self-breeding. Their ship-home sprang through space as if hitherto it had been tethered. Suddenly, the views on their screens could be magnified many thousand times greater, their listening devices so tuned as to be capable of picking up sound from light years away, the surreptitious slide of a plant out of its bulb and up through the soil. At a whim they were able to home in on any spot in any part of the perpetual spaces, be party to events they would never reach in millions of lifetimes.

Suddenly with one exception. Suddenly they had no control. The object of their journey was closed to them. For centuries the white blaze that was Altair had loomed up before them but now they could no longer see it, no longer knew if it was there. Like a blindfolded lightning bolt their ship hurtled on, they were lost but suddenly they were careering into the light of Altair washing wide, striking lesser worlds, striking and impelling the ship. At a planet blushing pink they slowed. They were cruising down through rose coloured skies. They landed in a grassy valley bathed in soft pink light, by a water's edge, disturbing birds. The grass was coloured pink. The soil was pink. They had decided to name this world Venturia Two. In the event, they could give it no name at all. They had come to a world much at variance with the world from which the ancient signals had sung. They found themselves mingling at their ease with people physically no different from themselves but not merely capable of magic but of creating worlds, altering worlds, rejuvenating worlds old and dead. They found flocks of red ships, many larger than their own, able to render themselves invisible, travel at speeds which made their own bolting passage a standstill.

The pink planet bathed through its days in the waves

of Altair, its star-sun, its nights in the radiance of four moons. Tiny volcanoes studded its surface, and when nights were cold an array of creatures were drawn to their warmth as on Earth they would have been drawn to water holes.

No questions were asked. None were needed. The pioneers knew where they were and with whom they had come to dwell.

The Supreme God and His Minions.

They were wrong. This was an outpost. They boarded red ships. At the speed of thought they flew to Canopus, a smiling giant two hundred light years from their ancestral homes. A mighty God indeed. They were with the God Supreme now and filled with joy.

They were wrong. This was an outpost. Others joined them. They streaked to Rigel, seen from their ancestral homes in the constellation Orion.

They had come to a place of blueness. Blue mists swathed their feet. Lambent blue flames licked their legs but they were immune. Luminous columns of blue smoke rising from the flames disturbed the high skies, alive with short-lived blue sparks. Blue lightning smashed over their heads.

The skies stilled.

They stood in dreadful silence. They waited, trembling. All joys were curbed. A deeper quiet descended. Mists and flames stilled as if frozen. They could do no more than wait, timorous in every quivering limb.

Sapphire sparkled in the blue mist at their feet before them, gushed high as a mist of sapphire stars into a pillar of sapphire flame, took human form.

They cried out and ran away. Sapphire flames seethed and billowed about them, forced them to be still and feet embedded in Rigel's heart, the Sapphire Human Flame strode to meet them, reach out to them, smile on them, call them to him.

Calming their nerves, they went to him. To this glorious culmination of all human destiny. The end of the human search. Unfaltering faith had been rewarded. They were in the embrace of the Guardian of the Gateway of Heaven. They knew! The human projection of the Creator. They knew!

The Guardian smiled, stroked their hearts, his eyes of sapphire flame entered them, lit their souls, licked from their eyes, it was as if there were no distinction between Himself and they and waves of sapphire flames about them blossomed into an infinite vastness and there were lights throughout them and all about them, lights upon lights, of consciousness, love, peace and they were part of those lights, enshrouded by love, absorbing that love, and peace of love filled all about them and all within them.

The Guardian smiled his blessing, shone his pleasure, sent them back, he had duties for them.

As the great sapphire beacon sank down into its pyre, the red ships sprang into space once more.

None among the pioneers were able to speak. But with gasps, arms were pointing. There, beyond Rigel, an arch of crimson, gold, turquoise. Pulsing waves of emotion throbbed feelingly to immerse them. Rays of Pure Consciousness, of the Fountain of Life, of the Birth of Eternity. Rays of the Truth.

Triumph ran amok.

There, at the apex, a light. A white flame as to a candle. Infinitesimally small. A flame of conscient energy.

Of the mother, the father.

The Cradle of Existence. Of Boundless Time. The Womb of all that had ever been and ever would be.

The Womb," Quita's pixie eyes flooded, "that had borne impossible disturbance. An embryonic spirit of awakening. The Creator.

Once more to the world of pink under Altair they sped, in their proud contentment settled into their new lot, took up their watch on the heavens on the Creator's behalf.

Their watch would linger parochially on that region among the galaxies to which they had belonged long ago.

They would be watchers of an unfolding drama, a cause for heavy hearts when its last act was played.

CHAPTER FIVE

"Human harmony on Earth would typically be a souring dawn. In inconsistent procession, man disentangled from his pre-human forebears into genetically a uniform species multiform in accordance with history and situation. He remained through long ages dependant on ancestral wits and skills in partnership with the orchestrated mobility of his family. Food gathering settled into stable food production. Family enlarged into community. Differing topographies, climates, soils and so forth dictated further divisions. Stable community flourished a banner of ethnic identity, tribe, and territorial claim but fate the ultimate decider, and nature.

Nature can provide only limited resources in any given area. Limited amounts of productive soils, water, grazing, animals to hunt, wood, space itself. Communities traded, by that enhancing the general well-being but the cult of individualism rose into being and its companion belief in the better likelihood of an agreeable life by attaining high standing in the eyes of others. Self-significance was made a prime objective, in a return to ways of animals multiplied into an all-encompassing swamp of detriment as individual vied with individual, family with family, community with community over control of resources. Competition propagated ill-will. Control was gained. Control was taken away. The human strife had come, and the history that would repeat itself over and over, that once control is achieved it is sure to decline and be lost. The war path is unknown throughout the non-human world. Conflict had been known hitherto among the hunters only when vital survival interests of different bands collided.

Outwardly towards Asturia, Atlantis adopted a polite and amicable disposition: a mask for festering envy and craving for revenge. Asturians were the Hated Ones from the Atlantean cot.

Its bombardment by the flying craft implanted no humility. Atlantean war galleys and mercantile fleets roved intrepidly from sea to sea, waterside to waterside, seeking out and uncovering new routes and profitable destinations, never losing an abiding passion for the convenient riches of the Middle Sea," the stick marched a tattoo from Spain to Palestine, "setting up colonies and yet," Quita's head wagged disbelieving gravity, "a time would come when the very existence of Atlantis would be doubted! What better example of the futility of greed and vain ambition?

Advancing humankind as a whole achieved cultural change in organized societies, stretching out tentacles of trade, seeking advantage, claiming the means of betterment for themselves, forced to fight dissenters. Thus were foundations laid for nation states and their armies and empires.

Atlantis embarked upon aggrandizement, commerce its foundations, gaining sound footholds on coastal lands and islands of the Middle Sea and along the seaboard of this Americas, where appreciable deposits of tin and copper enabled Atlantis to stamp the age of metals on the world. The Age of Empires had begun.

Atlantis rejoiced in its elevated position and accrual of wealth. Asturia stood aloof, exchanges with Atlantis discontinued, negotiating compromise seeming to have little point. Atlantis must run its own course. Thus were the people of Asturia in ignorance of the intensity with which the people of Atlantis from cradle to death despised them.

Asturian hearts were uplifted when came a summery

day, when a delegation of princes of Atlantis landed to petition for the re-establishment of ties, to be allowed to make amends, to be taught better ways. They offered up their sailors to be policemen of the seas against piracy.

A glad hour of naivety. Trade missions of Atlantis and Asturia benefitted. Atlantis remained true to its word. Asturia dropped its guard. Teachers from Asturia rode the waves to instruct Atlantis. The resulting artisans and scholars allowed Atlantis, in Asturian eyes a new model society and firm hand against buccaneers, to embark on a civil and scientific programme.

The stars declared war! A meteor outstripping all winds plunged into the ocean between Asturia and Tamalfua! The friction of its speed burst the atmosphere into flames. Earth recoiled. The burning skies blackened, the sun lost to view. Unseasonal winter freeze-dried vegetation, crops. A sorrowful world spun on drunkenly, away from the smoky dribbles of light that were all that could be seen of the sun, easing year by year into a slowing tilt.

Asturia drowned, froze, ten thousand lives lost. It had a new geographical position. It was now the southernmost land mass.

These events its people shrugged off as unalterable facets of fate.

Came a summer's evening and the arrival of fingers of frost. Through the night, water froze in pipes and taps, streams, lakes, rivers. Apathetic neighbour agreed with apathetic neighbour that this was an extension of a cold spell gripping high country, unready for any other conception, for all their abilities their fractional movement away from their sun not yet perceived.

By morning, the cold was blanketing everywhere, penetrating, worsening, there was no escape. All vegetation withered. Water froze in deepest wells.

Birds fell dead from trees. Sheltered domestic livestock suffered visibly. Hailstorms railed, blizzards, black ice sheathed piling snows that trapped the people in their homes, their sciences of little help, airships frozen hulks, space craft finding it ever harder to land among the white hurricanes and drifts burying homes like coffins more and more. But the people of Asturia bore all of it stoically, ruefully looking ahead to the floods that would follow. They were not to know that this was a winter that would not give way to spring. Then their forests came alive with the cracking of splitting trees. The death hymns of the trees accompanied the people awake and asleep but still they held on to their optimism. Impotent flying craft could only look down with their instruments at Asturia's disappearance under the snows, broadcast running descriptions. Then the coastal seas froze over. Delusions were shattered.

Individuals, families, convoys left for the open seas in every direction in craft of every kind. As with their forests, the Asturian peoples were sundered. Wallowing among ice-jagged waves, unseaworthy craft went down. Flying craft scouted, ferried, dropped food, escorted and gave directions but overwhelmed by the wide dispersion and numbers. Overloaded, they could only transfer survivors of sinkings to any nearest landfall to take their chances. For the most part, Asturians could only strive to remain afloat, get to where waves and winds would take them, thankful if their feet touched whatever shore. Few went to Venturia. It was too small, and not necessary, there was room on Earth. For weeks thereafter, wreckage of craft and human and animal bodies dead and living were spewed ashore along shorelines of this land mass where we now abide, now called the Americas, like scatterings of leaves. Whole and broken families, injured, sick, orphans. This continent was not unknown. Some had reconnoitred it in person from the air but much of it, a forest of unbridled luxuriance, had been charted only in fragments.

Many decided to make out as best they could where they were, with fish to sustain them. Groups set off along the seaboard. When the last farewells had been waved, four hundred set their faces inland, lifted young ones onto their shoulders. They died, fell out, fell behind, lost sight of all others, strayed, as for weary week after weary week hatchets hacked blind, groping ways through forest, swamps, dark, dense, terrifying, treacher-ous, steamy heat, rains, smells of rotted death, attacked by mosquitoes, halted by fevers, accidents, exhaustion, the unknown, panicked by air and ground shuddering roars and cumbersome feet of archaic creatures deposited from Venturia, in sustained hunger, delaying starvation's finality by making simple spears but finding precious little to hunt, in a throwback to their most ancient past pouncing on small animals, toads, lizards, grubs, snakes. Had they been cannibals, they would have found no flesh to eat on any of their own bodies. They died in the eyes of families and friends too frail to deal with their death. An arrow from a thicket stuck quivering in a tree. Naked savages with bows stepped fiercely out of their ambuscade. Women shrank with their children in dread behind their men. The savages made no threatening moves. One stepped forward, smiling as if to calm their fears, gesturing them to come. They were taken to huts of bamboo by a river. For the first time since lost to memory there was real food, real food as naked women fed them with fish, crustaceans, larvae, other flesh, fruit. Naked children looked on. The men made shelters of bamboo and leaves for them. Women smeared their wounds with stinking ointments. Sick were given stinking potions, poured into their mouths from bamboo tubes. Not every treatment worked. But lives were saved. For many blessed days they rested, ate. Reluctant to move on. Beneath their kindliness, the savages proved shy but children played with children. Four families announced their desire to remain. The savages were pleased by that, as their guests foregathered to depart in a modest ceremony presented them with bundles of leaves, food wrapped inside, liana straps made them not a problem to carry, handed every man a bow and leaf-quiver of arrows with barbed bamboo heads. The Asturians, overwhelmed by such friendship, would never forget. Their lives had been saved. For how long? Which way to go? The savages conveyed them across the river on bamboo rafts. It proved difficult to wave goodbye. Which way to go? The question tried their baffled minds. Likely, the river would be flowing back to the sea. They chose the opposite course. Losing sight of the river. The sufferings returned through more weeks of exhaustion through more ensnaring jungles reducing them again to a stumbling straggle but able now to hunt but inexpertly finding little edible game and making few kills but tapir, hogs, deer, alligators, monkeys, a giant snake among them and staving off Earth from famine, floundering through muddy waters, flesh bitten from legs by terrible fish, swarmed over cruelly by ants as large as rats, faltering frailly up a hurting slope, the emaciated ailing foremost an hour in advance of the emaciated ailing hindmost, out of the forest into better air but sinking, collapsing one by one, at an end, skeletal faces turning upwards, towards a sky blood-red silhouetting mountains, the aureole of an eclipse. Embrace of sun and moon crowned the mountains between two peaks. A woman's gasp was stifled by her hand. Through the spectral skies flew a ball of fire streaming silver ribbons. It scintillated through the red light between the peaks and into the love match of sun

71

and moon.

"A sign," someone whispered.

Hope breathed. They followed the comet's lead. A youth passed away. A giant bird attacked a girl on the morning of her wedding day, knocked her over a precipice into an abyss of rocks and whitening bones, landed on her body, picked her writhing flesh off her broken bones. It caused immeasurable distress. But hope, belief would not be subdued. A herd of vicuna merely looked on with curiosity as men surrounded them, exploited their indifference, struck down four to be food. More days passed by. All that time, sun and moon clung together. A goat trail fed hanging heads, ailing legs up to a saddle between the peaks attired in fiery hues from the sky.

They camped that night beneath a tumult of stars, sparks of eternal energy.

Through the next morning, their bodies fumbled downwards, by mid-afternoon into a water-laced vale of wooded downs, along a wooded bank of a brook into a scented dell.

Where they were hailed by Theus and Alorna.

CHAPTER SIX

"Opposites, Ilex?"

"Opposites?"

Sleepwalking, it was as much he felt able to muster, detached from himself. His voice and head not his own. They were out in the arena drinking orange juice and taking as far as he was concerned a long, long overdue break, rationality finding no room to breathe and worse, undermined by the infiltrating wish to be carried along, see it through.

"Yes, opposites. You have forgotten? Ilex, at times your head seems to be solidly blocked."

He took refuge in a long, slow as possible sip to her visible chagrin.

"Tragic disaster but such a turning point," she bristled, "a world-wide disruption of nature enforcing wholesale transferences of people, flora and creatures including fish." "The world can be a complex place," he muttered. He said it in Spanish to confuse her and put her off the scent of his lack of verve.

"Complex but necessarily so for the incorporation of nature's creative virtuosity," she retorted in mispronounced Spanish immodestly. "And you keep awake and take heed of all of it properly!"

It came with a dig in his ribs by her fist and scowled menace of more, upraising his listlessness into laughter and hiccoughs. Everybody else was moving but his knees folded him onto the ground.

"We will be last because of you!"

When she stalked away with a toss of her head the hiccoughs went from bad to worse.

Back she came bristling indignation. Both hands took him by his left ear, twisting it hard levered him to his feet and bundled him inside.

They were last by some minutes, walked the gauntlet of Quita's tapping toes.

"The two of you have been finding something better to do?"

The laughter of the audience boomed.

"Alorna and Theus waited by fires on which were standing steaming pots of meats and vegetables. There could be no mistaking them. Their statues and pictures were common possessions handed down. Tables held fruit. The water of the stream tasted more deliciously refreshing than any had tasted before.

A fleet of cylinders landed from Venturia, bringing food, grain and seeds. Their aching debilities tempted many to demand why more craft had not come very much earlier but they held their tongues.

Theus and Alorna abided for one year. They died side by side in the grass among flowers, leaving the Asturians and their helpers from Venturia working the threads of their fine new homeland into place. They named it Asturia, what else?

For one hundred years thereafter, old ways and expertise animated new Asturia capably. All thoughts of one day returning to their old home were eroded with every sighting of the white desert it had become, until it no longer mattered. They grieved for a while but buried their sadness in their needs of today. They would not forget it, and their city by the sparkling river and would always treasure its times but the past was the past and could not be retrieved, as a five year merry making visit by Calysos and Dintia underlined and superabundant harvests. Asturia came to mean beatific home once more.

Near reaches of the galaxy rocked to a monstrous detonation. Giant Jupiter heaved and boiled,

74

disappeared behind a monstrous blanket of smoking thunder hurling out a barrage of waste as if intent on storming all the heavens. A hunk of waste hurtled out of the smoke and on a devastating course, missing Mars by a margin, their magnetic fields cannoning them apart. Mars lurched into suicidal convulsions to bring its dying to an abrupt conclusion. The missile flew erratically on, now in the direction of Earth. Again there was no collision but another near miss. Already slowing, its close passing of Earth brought the death dealing rogue to a slackening drift and it coasted to a rest, there to remain as a paradoxical, beautiful light and heavenly tribute to beauty and love. Its near miss spelt disaster. Whirlwinds of flames devoured vast regions. Waters boiled, ocean waves rose to monstrous altitudes, driven by almighty tempests smashed down in prodigious annihilations onto land, crushing islands and coasts into beds of seas, poured down through volcanic cracks to unleash typhoons in the planet's bowels and water fought in steam shrouded fury with infernos roaring up from the depths below, suvivors outlasting opening onslaughts to be sucked into the wars of boiling waters and fire, liquefied in an instant so immediate as to preclude any feeling of pain though they numbered many thousands who ran in agonized madness into the worst of the steam and flames and over cliffs into the earth their only rescue.

The living staggered out of Earth's ruins to stare at death from starvation. New Asturia emerged incinerated, littered with incinerated bones. Stoutly, those who still lived with minds that were whole enjoined themselves to look upon this yet another devastation as yet another oscillation of the pendulum of Creation's ebb and flow.

All but two flying craft were beyond repair. They flew off to inspect the damage. There was little that they could do, for anyone. All things are begun." Quita moved his head in an attitude of bleak regret and his aged frame sagged visibly. "All must one day end, fall away from existence, become as if they had not existed. Time would draw from its sheath a new living Earth. But nor would journeys away from Earth be as meaningful as before. Furthermore, for as long as they would continue to function, the home for the flying craft would always only be Asturia now. When they ceased to function, that would be where they would moulder. On its havoc wreaking career, the rogue offspring of Jupiter had extinguished Venturia. At some future stage, between the orbits of Mars and Jupiter, the detritus of the unknown planet's corpse would be dubbed the 'Asteroid Belt'."

Quita stood immobile, distraught.

"The nativity of its star of beauty and love brought Earth to where it is today. The sea rover island Tamalfua slipped beneath inrushing waves leaving a heritage of islands and atolls formed by her hills. Overwhelmed from above, crumbling into fragments which waves bore away, her foundations crumbling, Atlantis sank without trace, leaving behind a heritage of doubt as to her existence."

Ilex surmised it was the size of Atlantis that was doing the fooling. Divers claiming to locate it all over the place were finding different areas.

"Initially, the majority of Atlanteans won through. None took to an angry ocean in vessels fit for scrap but even they could only float at the mercy of such destructive forces, and the people of Atlantis too were strewn to the winds. The greater number did make landfalls, not a few all along the shores of these now-called Americas to be fisher folk, hunters, farmers, vagrants and some became again traders, amalgamating with native peoples and applying the skills gained in their long-ago yesteryear and ascending to pivotal eminence."

Olmecs? Maya? Ilex jumped in, unprepared when he thought he could no longer be. Olmecs established their civilisation twelve hundred years before Christ, Mayans two centuries later and achieving high intellectual enlightenment and they had lasted two thousand years, created pilgrimage centres and city states comparable to Greece in cultural accomplishment and administrative acumen, one city had been twice the size of Rome, sapped by trade wars...

"Why do you not make a list then stand up and sing it out?" drilled into him.

"Why are you being nosey?" he flashed in Quechua.

"When I am your wife, I will teach you all about nosey."

She met his glance smugly, once more the winner.

"Astutely, a small host headed by Atlantean hierarchy ventured into the interior, eyes ever upwards. The years had passed and without contacts but the continuance of a dynamic Asturian community, somewhere, had always been known, their flying craft had been spotted. The rancour of antiquity reigned but could be shelved. If the Hated Ones could be unearthed, perhaps the problems of beginning all over again could be solved. If they could be found.

A cylinder found them. Asturians, searching for stock and crops to bring to their aid, and ferrying stricken humanity to locations far from their home, suspected trouble makers not on the same landmass, pleasingly transported vipers of Atlantis into their nest.

Theus and Alorna arrived as if summoned with singleness of mind and endeavour, injecting ideas. All belts should be tightened. If one were hungry then all should be. The flying craft were despatched on missions of reinvigoration. Fauna and insects of arid lands, hyenas too, were released on Asturia's ash dust. Desert vegetation, seeds, plants in flower, bees. Rabbits and small horses to crop shortest grass and for meat. Two pairs of sword-toothed cats. Living on entrails required kills every day and the rotting carcasses drew and fed others as only they knew, stimulating the life and organisms trapped by the hard shell of baked soil and bulbs and seeds which would have stayed dormant for years were given new cause as the strange, imported creatures disturbed the harshness and Asturia flushed with a grappling melee of fresh vegetation inside a year, to which a myriad of insects and more responded, bringing others which fed on them.

At the end of that year, Alorna and Theus passed away as they slept on their roof beneath the moon.

A resolution was decided upon. In tribute to something so deeply a part of them, their new home was renamed Venturia. 'Asturia' would linger as the southern polar desert.

Omens augured well. The seasons settled down. Shooting stars laced nights as if manifestations of supreme patronage. The harvests of the third year filled storehouses to bursting. Their resurgent prosperity encouraged and enabled the people to reinstitute their sciences with invigorated aspirations. Exhumed from memory, soon an airship was under construction. They would use it to begin a detailed plot of the world. The viper raised its head. There were riches to be plotted, avenues of trade to be found. A new space craft was planned, though old and young alike could only muse in near-disbelief upon a by-gone heyday for travel, and it was increasingly difficult to keep the two ageing cylinders left to them flying. A council of volunteers was formed to plan the forthcoming years, the Atlantean viper sowing seeds of subversion, grooming egos, gaining sycophants, planting schemes. Their garden grew dissatisfactions, unsteadying the community, alternative suggestions, squabblings. The first blood spilled by two brothers in an argument over what to do with a field.

None had knowledge of a burst of energy far from their doings. From a glowing planet sixteen light years distant, a red ship lifted off. From Canopus another. Out of the constellation Aquila they flew, too swift for any eye, alighting on a planet moon of Earth's sun, which, although once suspected, neither instrument nor eye could detect. There they were greeted by immortalised crewmen and women who had so long ago gone in search of it, and their passengers filed down into homes beneath Vulcan's crust.

Came an autumn night with the cereal harvested. Stars and fires dotted sky and land. The people were at rest after days of travail. Shouts roused them and tongues of flame. Assassins had played their hand, the councillors garrotted. Food stores seized, the flying craft immobilized. Axes, spades beheaded. There was no resistance. The people had no resistance to give. The mutineers were the only organization. A reign of unbending oppression was imposed, takeover of property, body and life, ravishment of women and girls snatched away to be chattels, livestock butchered in entire herds to be served in the weeks long orgy that followed the coup.

The new king was Aandi. Aandi ruled with evil sadism of Hell, with Venturian adjutants as links in his chain of command as minor overlords, told to take what they wanted as their rewards, and they did so. Scientists and engineers ordered to redouble their efforts to construct the airship on pain of death for their families. Death squads patrolled, the people directed to walk with heads bowed, blinded with hot pokers for daring to look a master or mistress in the eye, limbs sawn off and fed to their own dogs for the mutiny of failing to immediately obey, to serve as a warning men and women of advancing years and deemed to be of no value pegged out and left to die and rot unless eaten alive or dead by prowling packs of insatiable rats growing fat.

The viciousness of their downfall deadened the people. Self-accusation locked the gates of their minds. They had been tricked by their own self-deception into thinking themselves exceptionally placed, that they were not a benumbing wound into their souls.

A woman threw off her heartbreak and prayed. She did not beg. She demanded.

The words had not left her lips. A whisper swooped, visible only as it settled. From the great red belly marched grim soldiers in gold. They said not a word, all resistance summarily crushed, captives freed, remaining Atlanteans and Venturian collaborators rounded up and caged.

When it is over, the grim soldiery returned to their ship. But the great red hull stays. Quaking, hushed, Venturians gather near it, speculation seeping through the shock of their experiences as to who the soldiers might be. All approaches to them have been met with the stoniness with which the campaign had been waged.

Silence enwraps them. Not a bird sings. Not a bird, cloud nor breeze flies. They wait in apprehensive suspense. A ramp in the hull is lowered. The febrile stillness broken by unexpected sound. Music. Figures appear, taking stock of the crowd. Not soldiers this time but women and men in colourful robes. Hands wave. Voices call. The people are dumbstruck. They are being called to in their own words. Recognition releases gasps. So unlike the taciturn soldiery, these are one and the same! Gone are the warlike accoutrements, now they are swathed in soft, flowing raiments, are human and humane. Waving, calling, they hurry down, at the base of the ramp pause again, laughing and smiling into faces clamouring uncertainly to greet them. In a concerted move the rush is completed in a spontaneous outbreak of unfettered joy.

For eight days, orchestrated by a red headed couple, merry making submerges the people in unbaiting pleasures, the people asking no questions, their saviours offering to answers, enjoying instead each other's company like long lost brothers and sisters. Of that there is more than unvoiced suspicion.

A fine dawn cleanses the east, drives shadow stains of night into trickling retreat. The partying is done but continues as a tumult of happiness converges, in anticipation and answering a telepathic summons, rescuers and rescued clasping hands.

A blood orange sun climbs out of the eastern horizon into the very peak of the blue heavens. Where it hovers. There it stays. The assemblage stands before the red ship, Venturians in fearful suspense.

Earth has ceased to turn. The sun holds them in view. Astonishingly, stars emerge to suffuse the day face of the heavens with silver. The hour is dream-like. There are no sounds.

All wait. Venturians expectant, afraid. The ramp is lowered. Within the ship an ethereal sapphire glow pulsates. It flourishes, blossoms, issues from the ship to float in the air, jets high as a sapphire flame. Within the great candle a figure is suspended. On either side, lesser transparencies shimmer into being, in crackling gold take human form.

For some it is too much, they want to flee but new friends re-assure them and they are held by the press of the crowd.

The figures in gold are male and female. The centre of all attention may be either. All three hang motionless. They seem to be gauging the assembly as if waiting for the

moment, the mood. Then an embracing voice rolls over them, softly resonant, warmly pitched. The voice of a mother, a father, a dearest friend, of one of them, gentle but echoing to every reach of the sky.

"Loved ones," it accosts them, "your distress caused distress to us. For longer than you can know, we have been with you, accompanying your voyage through the eternity, desiring only the life you were given. While others betray their promise, you have been steadfast in the truth of yourselves and of the pureness of which all are made and capable. While others seek acclamation, though in your hands you wield command of that corruption, you have failed to consider it. You have been selfless whatever the temptation or adversity. While others have sought out every looseness of morality, you have not. Nor have you taken unjust advantage

"Purity and truth have no digressions, no conditions. Many doors are closed and obstacles lay against those who seek them, difficulties and wrongs which you have overcome. Even when they discover it, only a precious few throughout the forever will clasp the truth and not drop it. You are of that few, convinced of the true immanence throughout this Universe and all, the precious few who walk with the code set into your souls, who have not failed us.

"Hear my words. Be who you are. Hear my words. For they are your words. Be faithful to who you are. You will know troubles. Walk on. A lifetime may hold woes, nothing more. Walk on. Trials will afflict you. You may not recognize those trials. Walk on. Be sad. Walk on. Know pain. Walk on through whatever may beset you, whatever pains and sorrows, whatever gladness. Your trials will take many forms. Walk on.

Hold your heads high. Know that you continue to deserve our blessing. Be noble. Be true to the truth. The truth requiring no demonstration. Then will the Fires of Eternity burn for you. That is my solemn oath to you.

"Your loved ones taken from you salute you from their firesides in the abode of the blessed, your own future shelter as of the past, so do not be sad, nor for them.

"We leave you now but we will be with you, when you are here and when you are our companions in the realm of the spirits, in all its gardens of honour and love, your ancestral cradle home.

"We leave you now but we will be with you. Only remember the most beautiful gift that all can possess is the gift of selfless peace and harmony. We leave you those who will be your protectors and guides throughout time. You may see them as the epitome of human frailties. The trials may be for them as for you. You may see them as another burden but of them you will have need. Only be faithful.

"This Earth will be reborn and again, as if has from first birth. Self will conquer its human content. Many will promote themselves to gods, forgetful of the frail swiftness of their passing from nothing to nothing. They will awake from heir Forever-Night only once. Nor will they find you.

"Here in the world of flesh, there in the realm of the spirits, we will be yours. Uncountable lives you will know here and among the stars, as through the ages past. Only be faithful. Be true to the truth. Be at the peace which binds you into our hearts. Your presence is pleasing. Farewell."

Not a ripple stirs, not a kiss of breeze the air. Time holds its breath. All thoughts are stayed. For untold beats of the heart, the ever-changing cosmos changes not.

The spectre retreats, contracts into a flicker, returns into the ship.

None among the dazedly awestruck move a muscle. All are clasping hands.　　　Someone lifts his head and murmurs. In a deathly hush, all are held once again.

High across the sky floats a ship of burnished gold, rays of the sun like flights of javelins dancing off its gilded hide. Rain falls. In silence absolute, veils of lightning cleave down from the ship. The soil beneath their feet quakes as lightning pours onto the cowering land in vast unending currents. Horizons are in movement, germinating wave after wave of mountains. On every side is cause for terror, despair, a wrath of lightning, horizons aspiring to be mountains but the people stand immune. In no fear of anything now. A tribe of nomads negotiate their way into a mangrove swamp. Their scouts have found good grazing that comes next. As if timed with their first footsteps into the swamp, trees toss and writhe, winds strike with chaos and belching molten rocks a terrible living growth bursts upwards from the quagmire and up through the winds, overwhelms their terrified eyes. The nomads withdraw in haste. Earthquakes sink a zone, rend open a joining fissure. Rain fills the ravine with down rushing torrents. When the shores of the lake are established, the Atlantean prisoners and their stooges are marched into the red ship.

The space soldiers take their leave. The ramp closes. Soundlessly the red vessel rises, rotates on its axis to fly slowly away. It returns, flies slowly over the people. Like a pinched out flame it is gone.

The golden ship works on until the world is untrembling once more and skies azure. The land that is Venturia has been encased, not entombed. It is now a world within a world but apart. Its seasons will be its own. Its days, its days. Its nights will know the lights of the heavens. Spring will charm and renew. Summer warm and ripen. Autumn will pluck heartstrings with its saddening colours. Winters will be stern. There will be rains. There will be storms. There will be sunshine. There will be sun."

Quita nodded at Ilex, thoughtfully amused.

"There will be sun. The people stand in sunlight now. But sun, moon and stars will be memories between periods of glad re-acquaintance. A veneer has been cast. The extrinsic natural lights of the world and its heavens will flow through but, distorted by its mountains and their elements without and within, it will shield Venturia from all prying eyes, even of those who fly.

The golden ship glints as it tilts, aiming its nose at the highest reaches. It too is no more.

Only now do the people realize the red vessel has left six figures dressed in gold behind."

With a nod at them all, Quita stomped out of the room.

CHAPTER SEVEN

"Any more?"

He leaned heavily over the dog pen, tormenting Bruce, winced as the teeth sank into his hand and were slow to let go.

"I am being told," he ransacked himself for words, "that I am standing in some kind of hybrid Eden experiencing its share of setbacks but otherwise generally wandering sweetly on between naps in some fabulous tomb?"

"I do not like when you are being cynical."

He shook his head; a broken jigsaw seemed to rattle inside.

"How can I not be cynical?"

And yet he was feeling less than mocking, as if his punch drunk brain really had thrown in the towel and really was changing sides.

"But at least it is not the South Pole. So this riddle," an arm waved, "is Venturia. And you are Venturians."

"We. We. Others have been granted their own spaces. It is fair."

"You sound as if you are taking questions? Hang the flags out. Those caves I came through."

He forbore to mention the bones.

"Our centre of administration until we were able to relocate it permanently here. The Atlanteans too have used it, as you have seen."

"You re-located it out of the way of those apes. Where they do they fit in?"

"At once, the new waters teemed with newly created life, and soon every new land was a home, by virtue of the new creation and transported in. Though extinction is the final conclusion for us all, extinct were granted small existences afresh, lending the people a window to all that has ever been. Primates were transported and, largely from where you call Africa, classes of ape-human families, or else resurrected, primordial generations and subsequent primal human lines. Some have become quite a mix. Many of them took very naturally to your giant trees for ancient reasons of self-preservation, certainly when they encountered ancient enemies. All of them are worth preserving, do you not think?"

"I have not always thought so. And the very big one I thought I saw?"

"You did see. A genetic freak. There is more than one. The mightiest is always king. But are they freaks? After all, even they are not cramped in trees such as those, and do we not all tend to respond to every aspect of our surroundings?"

"I am to mine. I am becoming as nutty as you. No. Shut up and listen." He forced the effort to re-assert himself. "As you keep telling me to, I have been trying, and I mean trying, to take on board much too much that does not make sense. Yes, we have been here before, nor do I see it being the last time and, as you keep hinting, I can be pretty dim and in truth I often am but I can work things out if I have something to go on but what do I have to go on here? Nonsensical words from you and a nonsensical lecture."

He waved at a fly distractedly, beaten down by the happy emeralds. They widened in scornful amazement.

"Yes, we have been here before. How many more times? Be quiet. Now you listen. Are you where you are, or are you not? Are you here, or are you not? Have you experienced what you have experienced, or have you not? You are not kissing the ground and calling it 'home' but I do not see your tongue bursting to say no, and why is that? Instinct is why, and your faith in that

87

instinct. Has faith not been mentioned? The blind bat catches its flies and misses all obstacles with its radar and instincts and its faith in its radar and instincts. The callow blind bat on its first night out and about is you. Faith in an instinct is confirmation of the instinct, eradication of every last obstacle of doubt. Ilex, we are not counting upon you to follow your instincts as decidedly as the bat about any of this. How could we expect it? The learning process for a human needfully involves more than any bat's, and to question something outside our experiences is wise, and very human. Questioning can be a saving grace, help us dodge pitfalls. I expect there are aboriginal hunters outside now using rifles and their fathers still using spears, and some of those fathers find rifles impossible to believe even when they see one being used. So I ask you: is it the father or is it the son who, according to you, is the one that is nutty?"

His eyes rolled in supplication and away from the cheeky green happiness.

"Right. I am taking myself off the hook and away on a good long hike to take a good long look at things I know are real, and try to clean out my brain. That should please you. Come, dog."

"It pleases me. Have your good long hike, if you can in five minutes."

"Five minutes?"

"Or you stand to miss the best day of all. Unless you have changed your mind about marrying me."

"Are you telling me it is today? I must be the...."

"My goodness! You are the number one grumbler! Our wedding is tomorrow but we must prepare for it, at least you do. And for tonight."

"I cannot keep up with you," he muttered.

"As usual," she chimed.

"So what about tonight?"

"There are things we miss and considerably but not tonight, nor tomorrow the sun."

"The sun?"

"Yes, the sun." Her furrowed brow examined him with anxious curiosity. "Have you forgotten it? And after all the times you have been going on and on about it? Are you asleep in there?" Her knuckle rapped his forehead. "Hello? Is anything in there at all?"

It brought a chuckle from them both as he caught her wrist and hung onto it pleasurably.

"You know, Ilex, I am sure that Mata is going to have babies too. Look at her. Have you noticed? I am sure they will soon all be spoken for when people get to hear. I think I will ask a woman to keep an eye on her, then when they are born the news will get around."

"I can imagine."

"Now you listen to me!" she fizzed through clenched teeth, finger at his chin. "Men are bigger gossips than women! Get any men together and tell them anything no matter how ridiculous, and the next thing you know those Greeks will have another topic to philosophize about!"

Whereupon he scooped her up and over a shoulder, and with her thrashing hysterical shrieks in his ear ran into the complex and hurled her as far as he could into the pool.

"Ilex! Your hair! The rest of you will have to do but your hair is only a mess! Come here and quickly!"

He slouched over, shoulders hunched in mock regret.

"Stop acting like an orangutan. This is no time for it. Honestly, it is like trying to get a naughty boy ready."

Pushing him onto a stool, she fussed and fluttered about him with busy brush and comb.

"You touched upon the sun."

She ignored it. Meanwhile, his hair was no different from usual.

"No different?" She stamped her foot. "It is even worse than usual!"

"Hey." He held her waist, held her still. "What is it?"

Her chidings were usually delivered with some playfulness. She looked away, all about her.

"No..." she wrestled his hands.

"Not until you tell me."

"I cannot."

"Another riddle? Another bit of the jigsaw of nothing that fits?"

"It will be for you to see if it fits tomorrow. Do you not prefer to see?"

"Not if you are telling me you love me."

"Oh, Ilex," the emeralds embraced him into her bewitching poetry, stroking him, honing his senses, stampeding his pulse and unfettered elation to another peak, "I could tell you it a million times and a million times again. Would you not tire of it?"

"No."

"Listen. I want to tell you something." Her voice was a zephyr delicately stirring leaves. "My all belongs to you, only you, has loved you and longed for you through lifetime after lifetime of feeling loved and unloved, knowing bliss and only heartache and deepest loss. I ask no favours, do not beg but want you to share your all with me always, without fearing that you are imposing, a nuisance, a bully, a coward, and I insist that you never see anything you may do or think as weakness. I love you. I love all of you, and all that you are, and shall from the bottom of my heart for as long as the fires of our eternity will be lit, and after, were there to be an after or not. Now I must hurry. You are going to have to do."

She had said she must hurry but the time that went by denied it. The familiar feeling of being far away from himself mingled with his reluctance to impose any more strains on his ability to reason. It brought relief. He could not see himself leaving here now. But what price?

He crossed to the mirror. The first thought he had was the usual one, of a Viking minus beard. His father had been Welsh. A typical Celt? Had it been Herodotus who described them as muscular and fair? His father had been that, not tall, so what the mirror was showing was probably also a Celt but taller. And whatever and whoever the origins, he approved of the bronzed athlete with long fair locks, in a thigh length yellow lynx frock, yellow cape and sandals looking pleasingly back at him.

"You conceited thing!"

The cry made him jump. She tiptoed into the mirror behind him.

"If your head becomes any more swollen, you are going to be jammed down here. Ilex, honestly, I had no idea you liked yourself so much."

"I give up," he protested sheepishly. "You said I would do, and here I am only agreeing with you, and still I am in the wrong."

Anything else he might have said was knocked out of him. She too was in yellow, a halter and skirt slit down the thighs to above her knees, yellow leather sandals no more than soles with one strap across the foot. A yellow topaz necklace and comb in her hair were her only decoration, and the green jewels sparkling, the grin of her strictures. She was spell binding, breath taking, a sensation he would never grow used to. The impact of her now was the same as the first time. The same, he lit up, as every time. The same as always.

91

He must truly have gone mad.

"Come." She took his hand.

"I love you," he blurted.

"The feeling flows from me to you more than all the waters of all the rivers and seas put together and wherever they may be."

The evening was another bombshell. He gladly shed the tears. The skies were a tide of roseate and vermilion, saffron, silver and there, there, there white crystals that were stars, whiter stars than he had ever seen, the milky way more milky. It required a serious effort to wrench his weeping away from the stunning cabaret to look at this woman, her emeralds huge and glistening. She and this night were the perfect pair.

They strolled arm in arm among others. The entire populace were star gazers this night.

A breeze swirled formlessly. The entirety of the evening, its every star and colour, seemed to move away, leaving plumy trails. He could feel her vibrating. She made a small sound. And there, out of the mountain he had come by a golden, giant full moon seemed to bound up to join the phalanx of stars so gloriously bright, so clear and near he felt he could touch it, found himself foolishly trying to make out the footprints of those who had.

The rapture was immense. All night they stayed beneath it, and once the moon had reached its high point it remained. As if ordained to.

At an imprecise moment, a breeze rattled leaves, the air took on a chill, the stars lost their shine. A dog barked. A bird unleashed a chattering yell as if startled. Like a flower robbed of its bloom the moon faded.

The east showed the faintest diminutive pallor on the black velvet, slowly taking on a modicum of luminescence.

Stars were melted by it. Blue and silver javelins lanced across the eastern horizon and struck for the west. In a sizzling flash the meagrest spot of gold had appeared.

It swelled into a thin crescent. Golden lights streaked from it through the last of the stars. Her tears spilled onto her face and moved, he was following the path of the fiery God-star implacably driving the final vestiges of darkness away.

The relief was indescribable. His bride-to-be was holding him oh so carelessly now. It brought it home to him forcibly how much he had missed it; but how much more had these?

He heard her awed whisper. "Think on it. Our own Divine Light quickening our own Divine Garden."

As if in salute, undulating flights of birds sped beneath it. He wondered where they were going. Wondered if any of these people were inwardly begging to be as free to go where they pleased. His people?

Temptation to feel sorry for them passed at once. Life was a list of limited options, and when the choices apparently facing these were set alongside those being faced by an overwhelming vast majority it did not begin to compare.

His people!

A fist punched a palm hard and it startled her.

Eternity. Yes! He did not care if he was mad.

"Come, Rashida, Ilex."

The words intoned like omens of doom. Before them stood Settar, as unhappy looking as ever, beckoning them with his mace.

"Now is it?" Ilex rubbed his hands. "But what have you got to be so glum about? Are you being married as well?"

"Pa!" Settar stalked away.

"Try not to be a jester today."

Her hold on him tightened, her face had grown hard lines, the emeralds burned a more brittle brightness.

"Are you going to be such a tartar then?"

That their wedding would be a social spectacle had never been in doubt but with people falling in with them, hurrying ahead, converging like ants he wondered how many had ever had such attendance. They were obviously making sure it happened, he mused.

"A public execution," he quipped.

"This is a big day for them too."

"Why is that? Do they witness it being consummated? In some societies it has been a rule for wedding guests to stand by the bed and watch the newlyweds so they could see her blood and know she had been a virgin. She could be executed if she were not, and it made no difference if she had lost it to the man she had just married, and they used to get up to all kinds of tricks to make sure there was blood. But I cannot see all these getting a look-in, unless they form a moving queue or take it in shifts."

"You can be really base at times but let us see how long this flippancy will last."

His mischievous mood waned. For a supposedly happy bride on her supposedly happiest day something was amiss. Agitated waves of encouragement flowed from her but her thoughts too unsettled and complex to penetrate. He glanced up at the Sun, noticing others doing the same but the overwhelming majority ignoring it, showing typically short-term gratitude and he was as bad.

But her verdant orbs were trained unwaveringly on the arena into which they were heading, on that dominant plain structure. He had put it down ever since as a store or something to do with amphitheatre

94

activities, when he had thought about it at all.

It held his thoughts now, polished shiny white by the sun without so much as a scratch or bird's mess but marred by Semplar and Quita waiting in black by a pair of plinths like footstools at the centre.

Uneasiness found a place within him. His eyes narrowed. Butterflies laid eggs in his belly. He squinted at it hard. At a polished shell of a blockhouse. To keep people out.

The eggs hatched. His legs slowed.

Keep people in.

The hatchlings took off. The day was suddenly too hot but he shivered. The crowds were hanging back. Settar strode on ahead. Dark cloud seized the monolith, seized it from the sunlight, and Quita and Semplar. Flashes of purple seared his eyes, inside the cloud, from the whiteness at its heart, an imprisoned dismal ghost, irradiating the non- shapes of Quita and Semplar. Settar strode on. She was pulling at his hand, pulling him along. Settar strode without hesitation into the cloud and its purple fury. He tried to pull away. A premonition wrenched his lips. Superstitious terror numbed his brain but not to the stabbing black talons of fear. Death was waiting for him. He shook his head but death stayed. Would not be denied. He was shivering, sweating, cold, hot, still walking, Rashida flustered, trying to send him a bolstering smile. Purple flashes lit the indistinct figure of Settar as it halted at the indistinct figures of Quita and Semplar. Then he too was there, Rashida tugging him to a stop beside Settar, purple lightning smashing wildly all about him, within him. The lightning ceased, stillness, sunlight returned, his shivers making a liar of the restored sunniness.

Settar's arms lifted high, the sleeves of his robes hung like a vulture's wings. He broke into a gibberish harangue. His hand touched the white marble.

"My adoration is indestructible," her soundless electricity invaded his fluttering consciousness. The necklace jingled faintly as her squeezing hand rubbed his.

From somewhere came a muffled buzz. A section of the polished white marble swung upwards pivoting backwards into a recess. A sophisticated version of that crude little hatch on the ledge. He wanted to be there now.

A stage-like cavity was revealed, snow white, eerily lit by purple light. Empty. An emptiness which somehow was not empty at all.

Her hand had not left him but when he glanced sideways at her he was standing alone.

Settar's hand fidgeted. Up through the stage centre-left slid a glass case. It held for display, as if in a shop window, a model of an old man wearing the same black garb and grave features as the three counsellors, a wizened, hunch-backed giant.

"Kardan, our brother!" Settar called.

The sun struck the glass, caused the dummy to shiver as if coming alive. Its head tilted towards the sun. Cold feet stampeded up and down Ilex's spine. Settar's hand made quick movements. Three more caskets stood in line with the first.

"Semplar! Quita! Settar!"

They were too life-like again, all a little older than the living versions now. All three again only had eyes for the sun.

Ilex felt his legs weaken, his mind overhung darkly. Icy vigilance took him over. Another case, a second, a third, a fourth slid up as the exhibition's front row.

These three were different. Each held a man and a woman.

She was sharing his distress.

He flashed "Are we still being married?"

96

"Of course," trembled in his head.

"When?"

"Come."

Settar's vulture wings were flapping. The plinths were steps. All three old men were climbing. On the stage they waited, making space.

Ilex went first though his feet were in mutiny, clinging to her hand, icy, sweating. He was at the first case but looking away, at the sky, the crowd, Settar's voice grating, making him turn his head, in dazed revulsion finding himself close to their resolute stance, their eyes seeing but not seeing somewhere unknown behind him. No, they were seeing the sun.

She was a Juno in a calf-length violet leather tunic, auburn hair rested on muscular shoulders. In life she would have been fit, as an athlete perhaps a discus thrower or swimmer. With the waist of a teenager, the years sat upon her lightly though she had to be about forty.

The man she was all-but resting against was dark and muscled, in identical harness, sharp watching the sun through coal black eyes of a hawk. Violet leather strapped both wrists, calloused hands gripped a golden spear propping him up that was almost half blade, the black mane looked wind ruffled. The perfect male complement to the Amazon sharing his prison.

Ilex felt himself invaded by a creeping companionship.

"Machea and his Leona!" Settar intoned throatily to all.

Jittery, Ilex allowed Rashida to nudge his attention on, to a red haired young couple in crimson, both holding lyres as they beamed like Cheshire cats at the sun.

"Calysos and his Dintia!"

To a grey pair in grey smocks, a spindly man and

97

his plump partner, both sixty plus, unexceptional, only holding hands.

"Theus and his Alorna!"

Ilex focussed on them hard through swimming eyes and fog.

"We can move on," Settar's hoarse demand filtered. "The people are waiting."

"Come, my love."

Lost within himself but defiantly he let her take him on. To the next. Sighting on the raven haired, green eyed double of the woman beside him now. She even wore the same clothes. A blue rose in the hair in place of the comb. Holding his hand as she was holding it now, her body against his, claiming possession. Behind the glass, she lacked only the warm vibrancy he could feel coursing through the living version.

He hauled himself reluctantly with repugnance to her man. To the Viking, or Celt, hair fair and long, in yellow lynx fur, a short Roman style sword at his belt, at his feet a full quiver of arrows, leaning on a bow. A bronzed, tough looking hombre holding sternness at bay with the beginnings of a grin of near-arrogance. That cheered him slightly. But scars of cuts crisscrossed the arms, hands, legs.

In life he carried no bow, no sword. But the carbon copy of himself in front of him was exactly as he was now. He shook his head, made himself slacken. There had been plenty of time for them to come up with dummies.

"Ilex and his Rashida!" Settar's grating call interposed.

"When first you left us." The rant of doom grated closer like a crow homing in on food. "Underneath the tunic run the unhealing wound of the battle-axe that slew you, the left breast of Rashida bears its arrowhead."

The gruelling in-fighting inside his brain took on nausea, distress. It landed fully and sickeningly that these were not dummies.

That here was flesh.

Hers. His.

Old. Very old.

That out of these faces lit by the sun, death leered at him. Standing in the prime and splendour of pride in death was death itself.

His. Hers.

Behind the glass his jaunty stare, her serene dark beauty. A roaring grew in his head. Black hair never to go grey. Black hair that would only be black. No love in old age. No ever frailer kisses. No enfeebled mutual caring. He could feel death's arms already enfolding him, here and now but worse, they were reaching to enfold the quivering beauty beside him. Death shaking its fist at her and would not wait long.

Tense misery snapped. He rounded on Settar in tear blinded rage.

"Marriage by execution?" A paroxysm rendered him momentarily speechless. "Are you telling me we always die so young?" His wild anger rounded on Quita, gazing at him blandly. She was jerking at his hand like a bell rope. "Is this more of your warped sense of humour?" He snatched his hand free. All three old men were indulging him and making him all the madder.

"Ilex, there can be no doubt that you are you." Settar's squawking bony face looked as if it had found enjoyment for the first time ever. "You have lived longer, and for longer than you have wished for and you have objected to that also, not to your own infirmities but to Rashida bent and in pain, made more angry than you are now by your pain at the knowledge of her combing her hair and doing things to her face out of her love for you and her fear that her decay might, for only an instant, rob her of your love in return. There is much of the human in you but then, you are always born of a human."

Non-plussed, Ilex softened into suspicion, steeled for the next trick.

"Yes, Ilex, you are Ilex. Impulsive always, stubborn, truculent when confused, prone to anger and strong action, and it has taken you into misadventures. How else did you come here? How much of your admirable, reckless effort did you plan with sound judgement? You are one who will burst unseeing into any unknown, stand as unsurely as a newly walking child yet pure and defiant in the situation of your own making. To you, nothing is impossible but seldom do you work out beforehand that things may need more careful consideration, you are seldom prudent, much needs no more than the smallest spark to make you burn. In so many ways do you resemble the flames from which you are made."

Ilex could only look daggers but Settar had not done with him yet.

"Calysos brings comfort, Theus brings wisdom, Machea brings deliverance, a fighter, like you. He is resting now but a threat hangs in our air."

"Are you telling me that every time I am here there is a war?"

He nearly choked on it, Rashida tugging, Settar simpering. He rounded on Rashida but Settar held up a hand.

"You are like a child. Threat of a trial is always near. None may know when it may fall but were it to fall and were you to fail the people stand to be the sufferers, driven into no longer being themselves and it will be the end of them. The wisdom of Theus might go unheeded. Calysos would have us all die laughing. You

100

have succeeded."

"You mean I have failed?" he shouted.

He had forgotten the original argument.

"No, but you have on occasions needed assistance, though you do not give up. You have not done so yet. Your sentiments are human but your will is strong, and the test may fade before its final hurdles in acknowledgement of your will, and with Rashida you are allowed to live long and happily although, as I have said, you do not always like it when you enter old age whether from peace or war. None can predict what will come but Ilex, whatever will come your friends, these people, their children are your responsibility, not mine. Their fate rests with you. And this is a test for you now!" His wings flapped as he flourished his hands at the cases, broke into high cadence. "This Rashida, this Ilex, Alorna, Theus, Dintia, Calysos, Leona, Machea, the counsellors stand in their flesh and bones, not made by mortal hands. These people are your people, who will belong to their living future for as long as you demand that be so!"

The squawking tone lowered.

"They are or they are not. They will be or they will not be. Now, we must leave the tomb monument to allow the people to take their share of today, and I think we can arrange something that will lighten your temper, if you do still wish to marry Rashida, that is."

"Do I have any choice?"

Then the mausoleum and its contents were behind them. They were escorted to a purple carpet at the centre of the arena and asked to kneel side by side. The last thing Ilex saw was Settar's ankle as a blanket dropped over them.

A melancholic incantation broke out above their heads.

"Why is he being so miserable, I am the one under

101

here," he flashed giddily.

"Are you feeling better?"

The blanket fell away from them. Counsellors and crowd encircled them.

The right palms of the three sages reached to hang above them as Settar chanted something incomprehensible sounding like a foretelling of disaster. Then:

"May you live long and to advantage. May your union be fruitful. You are now man and wife."

CHAPTER EIGHT

"Now I am decidedly your wife, again," she purred the emphasis.

The wooden beaker of honey wine glowed warmth and comfort through his system. They were by their own fire in their dell, granted small semblance of privacy among the weeping willows and no others were camping this side of the stream skipping by like a playful string of pearls sharing the party but well-wishers thick and fast out of a pleasure land of other fires, music, dancing and laughter of a celebration that would have no set end. Cloth-covered trays of cakes and other foods and stone jars of juices, corn beer, wines of fruit and honey stored handily inside the hollow trunks were being gleefully pillaged, every gang of cock-a-hoop callers making Ilex feel somewhat the imported bystander because names he could put to faces were few while to a man and woman and a good many of the youngsters, their association with him was in depth and personal, he was brother, confidant, ally and best friend.

He absorbed her steeped pleasure into his own calm stimulation, eyes half-closed but not wanting them to close and lose the smiling loveliness permeating the very air with a supersensual and yet delicate spiritual beauty, simmering him in a deep well of emotional gratification. But...

"You must not let up in your teachings, and I want all the bad news. And I want Hadja, Atlantis, the lake under surveillance every hour day and night."

"How fiercely responsible. Lacking clear sight, you walk this unknown, potholed road impressively."

He could not respond immediately, let the words

choose themselves.

"Teach me."

"But not now."

He kissed her temple, unhurried, easing in his mind, furtively lifting the haltar to the frolic of flame lights over breasts and their nipples he would never see and touch enough and she held them for him to suckle, a spontaneous gift. Grass muttered and a mob whooped through the willows propelled by a manic drum. Food and jars came out of the trunks again and men and women of middle years were boisterous teenagers again as thirty or so drank and ate round the fire, twirling, weaving and interweaving with hoots of laughter to a lively allegro played on the drum and a hollowed gourd with plucked metal keys. A man climbed a willow; a woman encouraged him to fall.

Midnight had gone. The weeping willows were quietly stirring, stroking a velvet cloth sky inlaid with jewels in scintillating density, a giant moon of gold at its zenith. He was reminded of claims that diamond storms from space had bombarded Earth.

She languidly reached up an arm.

"Rigel," the shadowshine of her arm directed him unnecessarily, "Canopus."

There was no missing the two enormous diamonds cleaving their paths.

"I presume you know that Rigel is seen outside as part of that constellation," his hand traced its outline. "They know it as Orion the Hunter." His knowledge of stars was basically confined to ones that could be used for navigation but he suddenly felt inspired. "You can see the three stars for his belt, his sword hanging down. Rigel marks his left foot."

"Nine hundred light years distant, so we are seeing it not as it is now but as it used to be nine hundred years ago. Your hunter stands astride the celestial

104

equator and can be seen from most parts of the world. His constellation is a wealth of nebulae and stellar objects. Star patterns do not appear to alter perceptibly from year to year, and the groups we see now are the same as those that used to be seen by, for example, the pyramid builders of Egypt. The nightly, and daily, east-to-west movement of the sky is due entirely to the rotation of the Earth. It has nothing to do with the stars themselves."

"This child is aware of that."

"Stars are not fixed in space as if nailed. Their movements are individual, fluctuate at high velocities. Legends have classified your Orion as a hunter since early days of civilisation. Also, Sumerians associated him with their king Gilgamesh, and pictured him fighting a bull, which is the constellation Taurus. There. To Egyptians he was the pharaoh god Osiris, whose jealous brother Set, god of the forces of chaos and of the hostile desert lands, cut him into pieces, hid them in the box and floated it away down the Nile. The pharaoh's wife, Isis, found his remains and threw them into the sky. To your Greeks of old, Orion was, yes, your hunter and handsome, sprung from Jupiter, Neptune and Mercury, with the power to walk through the sea and on its surface but his love life tangled and troubled. He fell in love with Merope, daughter of Oenopion, king of the island Chios, and her father set him the task of clearing the island of wild animals as the price of betrothal. Orion did so and won his bride but his subsequent ill-treatment of Merope so angered Oenopion that he intoxicated Orion then blinded him. He regained his eyesight by exposing his eyeballs to the rising sun, and avenged himself upon the king but only to be killed while swimming by an arrow of Artemis, goddess of hunting and the moon, whose affection he had also won, out of her jealousy of the dawn that had healed him. Yet another myth says he won the affection of Artemis but Apollo, her brother, accused Orion of distracting her from her duties and tricked her into shooting him. When she uncovered the trick, the grieving Artemis honoured Orion by placing him in the sky. In yet another story, the Earth released a scorpion to sting him to death as punishment for boastfulness, and Orion jumped into the sea. Because of their enmity the two were placed on opposite sides of the sky, which is why the constellation Scorpius appears in the east as Orion sinks in the west. Humans crave consoling illusions, and so time after time myths, beliefs and gods are repeated and in disparate parts of the world. Early astronomers did build up some knowledge of the stars, and although they knew nothing about their true nature, the make-believe art of foretelling events by understanding the reputed occult influences of the stars on human affairs granted the forecasters considerable status."

"It still does. And Sirius? The brilliant white star left and down from Rigel."

"A star may appear brilliant either because it is comparatively near, as with Sirius, or because it is really very luminous, as with Rigel. Some see Sirius as one of Orion's hounds. You would think it worthy of more. Perhaps it is part of an unknown scheme of things since I have heard scarcely a mention of it beyond the interest of some who have made the stars their study."

"Canopus was also the name of a seaport of Egypt. What about the Atlanteans here now?"

Negative emotions persisted.

"Do not spoil now."

Taking his cue from the moon as it dipped, raw sensuality let the fire die, found her breasts, she rebuffed him urgently, fought him off, fought him down, straddled him with choking squeals aimed across the length and breadth of the night, he laughed into her hair.

Birds began to chink. In the earliest grey light she bathed in the stream and he waded drowsily in to wallow alongside her, his wedding night had taken it out of him but richly awake. From where he never knew, she produced a change of clothes, green gowns for them both. She carried a cloth knapsack as they drifted away in languorous high spirits, escaping early. They picked mushrooms in the dew. In the hideaway of an elder clump she cooked the mushrooms in llama butter mixed with yellow peppers produced from her knapsack. A sparrow landed teetering on the tip of a branch. Her hand, very slowly, reached. The sparrow hopped into her palm, eyes flitting between her stirrings and her face.

Voices left them alone. They settled in, a blanket about them, taking advantage. He cuddled her when she slept, when he fell asleep himself.

They awoke to birds bubbling. Whites of gulls called as they passed over, tinged by low rays of the sinking sun, a red-gold throne on a mountain. The elders wrapping in scented gloom. The heavens shining smokily. The fire ashy embers. He scattered a handful of dry grass, made a small heap of tiny twigs. When he blew into it, with a puff of sparks it glowed and flickered and, pleased with himself, a frame of bigger sticks carefully followed. He snuggled down beside her again, registering the gathering night, birds ceasing to sing but a descending peace coming vastly, movingly alive. The heavens ignited. Owls complained. Perhaps a fox barked. His fire sank to a red glow, no flame nor smoke but supporting the peace and his fulfilled peace of mind and the intensely fulfilling, mighty, spellbinding peace overhead, the dark leaves of the elders against stars to his left, Canopus their heart, to his right against the moongiant.

Her voice was again immodest. "Because of its brightness, star trackers often use Canopus for orientation. Canopus your seaport enjoyed very considerable trade with your Greeks but was notorious for its profligacy but gained extra importance because of its temples and tombs, such as the great temple of Serapis, a god of healing of Egypt who became a cult divinity in the Hellenistic mysteries. His worship spread to Rome and further but it is not easy to class him among the gods of Egypt as he was disowned by Egyptian priests because of Greek influence in his creation. After the conqueror Alexander added Egypt to his empire, Serapis was introduced by Ptolemy the First by combining the god Osiris with elements of gods of the Greeks, allowing Greeks and Egyptians to unite in common worship. Canopus your seaport was named after the helmsman of Menelaus, king of Sparta. Returning to Sirius, Egyptians were so bound up with the Nile's yearly cycle, when they realized that at their capital, Memphis, the river began its own rise at the rising of Sirius in the morning twilight, they took Sirius to be a divine star responsible for their river that provided them with much good fortune. Fish again."

She ended it boastfully sweetly, and she was right.

"How do you know all that?"

"Should I not know? Did we not know them all before they knew themselves? Those Egyptians have earned our admiring respect and could be our good example for, in spite of drastic changes of condition they remained who they were from a race of stone age savages breaking new ground to portentous culture accumulating significant knowledge and literary wealth, and when ages of all kinds of crises caused them to refashion, they survived fundamentally as themselves, did not change."

He let it pass on. "When that craft sealed Venturia in," he spoke against a bared nipple, "it was acting out a premise that this Earth was once a quartz bruised by hits from space, and the bruises formed the original basis of life. By an alteration of molecules, I suppose. Just a thought."

I. "And you think it a clever one but one thought you have not had concerns the identity of those first representatives left behind from the red ship, and you have ignored every hint. They were all four counsellors, and yourself and myself. You were Venturia's first king."

II. "And first dead one," he felt a cold clutch of foreboding, his mind failed to dismiss it, trapped in bizarre mud.

III. "Were you not bound to be?"

IV.

V. At Rashida's inclination they did their own visiting, falling in with playful campfire scenes translating into crystal clear recognition of the to-hell-with-losers rough and tumble he had left behind. Modern industrial economics, he concluded, and nature were fundamental enemies in a war which modern industrial economics could only one day lose but dragging everything else down with it.

VI. They sat by a pond, puffs of breeze ruffling it. Black and white wagtails pecked and picked over the shallow mirror. A grey heron stood as still as a stone carving on the other side.

VII. "What did I see in the caves?"

VIII. "Must you spoil now?"

IX. The heron was adding a degree of curiosity to the composition. Small fish and larger were everywhere so why was it doing nothing? Was it already full and standing there because it always stood there?

X. "According to you, I have mountains to climb. What you tell me now might save both of us from being overworked when the weather is against us."

XI. The green lenses took their camera shots of approval.

XII. "The first trials came within weeks. Some of our fishermen were killed, their boats taken, farms raided for livestock. You drove them away but in less than a year a large scale landing surprised us. It was Machea who put them down."

XIII. "Why not me?"

XIV. "You had passed on."

XV. His belly hollowed. "And they sprang their surprise from?"

XVI. "Hadja is one of twenty islands in the new lake. Once they were hills. They cannot be seen from our shore. The prisoners had been deposited on the islands without food or any other essentials but fish that followed the water into the lake provided a lifeline, and trees on lower slopes under the water were made into rafts and boats and went into the building of their first homes. Atlanteans can get along with each other, and do come together in a congress to attempt to discuss difficulties but it is thoroughly in their blood to be contentious and seek solution by war, but we must give credit for the fact that they not only pulled through but began to live well."

XVII. "The caves."

XVIII. "They fight civil wars but their most persistent quarrel is with us. Their aggressive hostility towards us has not been lost for a single day. When last they came, they had not bothered us for a little over two hundred years, and when you and I had known two long lifetimes here together, one after the other quickly and both times from when we were young. How I pray this is such another."

XIX.Rummaging in the knapsack, she passed him an apple.

XX."And, of course, we know each other between our unions here. What are called life and death can be a living and dying bliss."

XXI."According to the philosopher Plato, thousands of years ago a brilliant civilization existed on Atlantis but its people became corrupt, and so the gods decided to punish them, and explosions sank them. Plato's story fascinated people of later times, and various theories developed about its location and disappearance. Historians nowadays tend to believe Atlantis was an island called Thera, in the Aegean Sea, east of Greece. Thera used to be the home of the Minoan Civilization. Volcanic eruptions destroyed most of Thera and wiped out the Minoans, and this is what is thought to have inspired Plato's Atlantis. There are long standing predictions that it will someday rise from the sea. The caves."

XXII."When last they came, it was as if to make up for all the years they had missed. They herded many of the people into those caves. Stored them there. As food! The caves were made into a most horrendous pantry! They had become obsessed by the idea that by eating us they would gain all we have and are. The way in you found was cut by a prisoner attempting to be free. He was, and is, an engineer. He was caught in the act of making an escape, not caring about what awaited on the other side, and had he managed to get to it he would certainly have jumped, and others with him. Machea caused the chasm by an explosion as a bar to outsiders. He had already chased away one tribe that had climbed up. None are likely to get up there now."

XXIII."I did. Have you forgotten? I would have jumped if the dog had not found the hole and I had

111

found some courage instead."

XXIV."In the early human ages, courage and daring were not merely virtues but essential qualities if life and therefore the future were to be preserved. You have never lacked either, nor the strong streak of nonsense you accuse everyone else of possessing."

XXV."A barbed compliment from my wife?"

XXVI."Poor husband. You crave a proper compliment? Anyway, the poor engineer was found out, and because they had been shielding him, for punishment all the prisoners in that section were sealed in, and to make their end even more horrid they were left with tiniest quantities of food, and it was flesh of their own families and friends, to extend their sufferings and set them against one another. It pleases me so much that every one of them advanced upon death with dignity instead. The seal of their tomb was the barrier you met, which had partially collapsed and your dog found a way through."

XXVII."You knew that?"

XXVIII."Of course. Why do you sound so surprised? Ilex, why has so little of what Quita has told and shown you managed to get through? Are you not paying any attention? I demand your promise that you will apply yourself unstintingly! Mercifully, when he saw how nobly they were dying, the Great Guardian took them early into his palm, so gently they did not know it. It was good."

XXIX.The sights came ploughing back, stressed tenderness in her words magnifying the horror, and for the first time in his life he knew total, unalterable hatred.

XXX."How did I get in?"

XXXI."Initially, your hard working knife triggered an electromagnetic switch releasing a lock. The engineer shut the door solidly when he detected his captors were coming. Word had got out. Loose tongues in their suffering had betrayed him. Yes, Atlantis knows of it but not how it works, nor its measurements and location exactly. They have never hit upon the way of opening it. Very likely, by now that door is a fable, if in their minds at all."

XXXII."You know how to open it? From both sides?"

XXXIII."Of course."

XXXIV."The bear."

XXXV."A gruesome guard overseeing a gruesome playroom. Placed there to welcome every fresh batch of prisoners," both hands gestured pitiful strain, "awaiting terrorized turn to be placed on the menu, their living bones crushed, joints axed off, flesh cut off piece by piece and eaten and they were made eat their own families, wives, husbands, children, made to eat pieces of themselves cut off by their captors. Some were taken away in one piece not merely to be burned alive but cooked, boiled or roasted, slowly, prepared and tenderized on the altar you discovered. Flayed alive. Flesh salted. Yes! Salted! While still living! Still living! Who could wonder why so many lost faith! Who could ever imagine..."

XXXVI.Her expression shattered into suffering, pallid face squeezing tears, sweat jewelled her forehead. He hugged her hard, seized by the images, a grim wind.

XXXVII."It came close to guarding you from me." His mouth forcibly made light, her pathos hurting. "It almost gave me a heart attack."

XXXVIII."Then it is as well you did not meet it in the flesh."

XXXIX."We are in agreement."

XL."You forget how well I know you, that in yourself you do not know what cowardice is, no matter

113

how afraid you might be. Ancestors of the bear had occupied the caves after we vacated them. They went from home and sanctuary for us to home for bears, and for other creatures, I expect. They must be full of bats."

XLI."I do not remember seeing any. Nor rats." Should he have? All the way up there? "Hardly a sanctuary now."

XLII."It can be barricaded into an impenetrable stronghold. It would be better stocked with food first but water is not a problem and, as you so thoroughly learned, hunting grounds are not far away. In its heyday it was citadel, parliament, office, home for many and workplace, where much was considered, and brought to reality, and there are lesser caves and holes in walls containing archives and other proofs of our story and more, which Atlantis is not aware of. Yes, you came across some but even though you came the longest, wrongest way you missed much more than you saw. One could find out for oneself a great deal up there, answers to all your bothersome riddles."

XLIII."You want me to go back there? Thumbs down, for now. But you can give me one answer here and now. I have jumped into this with both feet. The reason is, I want to. The reason I want to is because, in very large part, I am willingly accepting everything I have been told, seen and heard, but the prevailing influence is you. I cannot imagine not believing you and in you. But added to the risk I am embarking on, which might very well turn out to be stupidity, is the fact that I have no remembrance whatsoever of any of this, or of any of the things I have supposedly been into up to my neck. Why is that?"

XLIV."As often as not you arrive clear headed and all-knowing but want of knowledge can be a prime constituent of the test of yourself, a deliberate blank. It is not a unique situation. You are not all alone in losing pages of your past. No matter how bygone times are woven with vivid facts locked into ancestral memory, as years elapse older colours fade or spoil out of true. Even most outstanding moments and figures become another unknown. But memory may give way to sentient instinct, which you showed when you berated poor Settar. For our people and you and I, the here and now is our past and foreseeable future state here on Earth. Throughout existence, fate is a chain of mysteries close-linked. Death is fate's arch-unknown. For humans, while Death the act is no secret, beyond it awaits fate's greatest and most petrifying, and for some alluring, mystery. So attracted by it are some, they spend their every living hour wishing it upon themselves. I am not referring to desperate suicidals but to purists applying themselves to its study who acquire the belief that it is nothing to fear but among them too, many, as they are moving into death's gateway but unable to see the other side, feel a need to hesitate, too late, concerned that their findings may be at fault? For you, Ilex, at this juncture the here and now is a greater personal unknown than is death and vitally so, and in need of your most unbending cerebration. You have reason already to be proud, as I am of you, for although you have many seemingly impossibly difficult, dark distances to travel and beset by your normal human frailties, you are confronting all, your doubts and misgivings, with your own perseverance, your own brand of personal courage, which is why it is you who sits here, yes, sometimes stumbling, with me. And I will say this and then please shut up. You are a good king..."

XLV."I have..."

XLVI."Ilex, shut up. You are a good king, always. On that first occasion, taking your cue from earlier actions by Theus, you issued your orders. The flying craft made their concluding sorties, securing a decisive spectrum of life, and humans thought worth saving, and placed them in regions that suited them best. In the blue mountains live a people who returned at once without ever letting go to the familiarity of caves. I for one would never choose to live in the frozen land but some with snows and ice in their blood were all smiles at being set down there. Others were placed again into swamps, deserts, jungles. On occasions, some of our own people leave us to dwell among some them, out of the sheer attraction. Some escape to the world outside. A wall imprisons as well as protects and they find confinement too difficult. The passage out is, indeed, the way you discerned, the way I took you to, strewn with hazards but straightforward to identify. As in every situation, everyone who thinks to escape is allowed a margin of human error but should they persevere sufficiently, suddenly there is not a way back to see. The passage closes behind them, and they have deprived themselves forever of their singular status but who is to say they should not? Sundry creatures now form a reservoir against future disaster, little matter what extremes of climatic and terrestrial changes befall. Carcasses, wool, blubber, waterproof skins, ability to exist with little water. And that, my cleverer-than- you-think Ilex, was your doing. Your foresight. Yes! In a similar way, should nature inundate us with misfortune in whatever way, we have people to fall back on whose skills will see us through."

XLVII."The flying ships flew out after they had been sealed in how?" he asked it heavily, the riddle indispellable.

XLVIII."The shield can be made to dissolve, in small part or in its entirety. Its outer side is all apparently of mountains but in parts an illusion, such as parts of your mountain. It means the gods can fly in whenever they wish. Fish."

XLIX.He grunted.

L.   "It is true! Machea always flies in."

LI.   "Machea flies. Theus and Calysos turn up out of the blue. I do all the walking."

LII.   "What would stop you being the number one grumbler?! Were you not flying when first you set out on your hare-brained schemes, using your father's words? Why? Are you losing your feet? You had the flying machines dismantled but stored. Rightly, you opined there could well be need of all skills on some future day, and all technologies can be resurrected, and scientific studies do not pause. The counsellors supervised the building of the new citadel. It was Calysos who arranged the building of Hadja. Who else? Hadja is comparable to your Canopus the mercantile port, for its fondness of a good bargain and sleazier side, and attracts more of our people than I can approve of, out of their own free will, lured by its novelty if only for a time but however short or long they can never come back. All who choose voluntarily to leave us are deemed to have elected to forfeit their eternal tomorrow, and this they know. Whatever might be the outcome, whatever any choose of their own free will, who can say they should not?"

LIII.   "I would like to know that Hadja is being watched as we laze about here."

LIV.   "You do sound so ferocious. Yes, soldiers are near discreetly, and the lake is fished. A wicked city. Or is it so evil? It does seem to suit a comprehensive number from every corner, including the too many from us but it draws them from us like a lump of jam used as bait for flies to get them away from one's dinner. Hadja is our link with Atlantis, as you have conjectured. Our boats use it as anchorage in gales, and land fish catches and other wares, or steer there for the more degrading forms of contact which Hadjans are willing to provide."

LV."You do not sound too sure that they are always wrong. The Hadjans."

LVI."Each to his or her own, as long as innocents are not abused. A whore, a brothel have their definite benefits and oddly, or not, the sexual abuse of an unwilling partner in Hadja is almost unknown."

LVII.He told her of some of the attitudes outside. She found much of it improbable.

LVIII."The version of Christianity dominating this South America is the Catholicism based in Rome."

LIX."You insist on repeatedly telling me what I know."

LX."Then you also know that as far as they are concerned, sexual intercourse has one purpose and one purpose only, and that is to procreate? Enjoying it is immoral, and people who do can earn severe reprisals."

LXI."Absurd. They evidently place great reliance on the distress of hand-to-mouth insecurity which they are able to manipulate, which is bound to follow such strictures, to sate a voracious appetite for domineering. Yes, this has been a pet theme of yours rehearsed over and over, and while it is true that in basic societies many children do help lighten the work load, and many births can compensate for many short lives, all of them have to be fed, and food is finite. A plague of locusts eats everything then they all perish. Making sure that women with scant means become pregnant again and again and with its twin underlying threat of persistent harm to her, let alone privation for all, is immoral, and those who impose such contemptuous tyranny are deserving to be punished." Disgust etched her. "How many of these domineering Roman Catholic priests make sure it is not they who labour morning, noon and night to look after their flock of children when they

118

marry?"

LXII."I thought you said you knew all about them. They do not marry. They are not allowed to. They are meant to be celibate, and must not even masturbate. Complete abstention is laid down as one of their keynotes."

LXIII."They are absurd from beginning to end. I would gamble, and not a long shot, that not a few of these moralisers brush their keynote aside when it suits them."

LXIV."Christianity has generally been like a pack of rabid hyenas, turning on one another for holding doctrines deviating only slightly from the rules of the moment."

LXV."The spiritual leaders of Islam, for example, do tend to be decentralized and work at the local level but by and large on common ground. Who call themselves Christians are hierarchic and factional, with an idiosyncrasy for divergent leaders interpreting their scriptures into divergent sets of rules, few of which their Christ would approve of."

LXVI."There used to be a big thing about witches. It left a lot of women wide open to abuse. A woman suspected of being a witch, sometimes she only had to be ugly, was thrown into water, a pond or a river. If she sank and drowned she was innocent. If she floated it was held that the water had rejected her because she was in league with the devil, and she was in big trouble then."

LXVII."I am sure. Illness can bring about disfigurement, and age is no friend of beauty, but Christians, we agree, are not alone in feting their gods as their banners and excuses for personal vile agendas. I could never bring myself to believe in a god as a man with a beard and halo. I am more than willing to believe in a god who loves, in the love of man for man,

119

for animal, bird, flower, cloud, a man such as you, because for myself love gives a meaning to life, and love is our god within us. For myself, that is you. Ilex, I stress, tear yourself away, root and branch, from all you know and think you know of every so-called religious faith of this world. Yes, that is what they all say to recruit and hold in isolated detention their supporters but I repeat and repeat: tear yourself away, stand apart. Ripen. Mature. Rivet yourself to faith in your here and now. Faith in yourself. In myself. In our cause and reason for being. Ripen. Mature. Be obsessed with faith, and self-belief. Celebrate it. Stand your ground."

LXVIII.Omitting all facts of the combat, he spoke of the Nazi establishment of the German Third Reich out of the humiliating Versailles peace settlement and dire economic depression, Adolf Hitler's barnstorming oratory and promulgated theories of the purity of an Indo-European race to which their own select Germanic people belonged and the therefore essential inferiority of other races, and consequent extreme sense of German nationalism and anti-Semitism, the adoption and imposition of Nazi systems and dogmas across Europe, the six million Jews and others incarcerated and exterminated in the concentration camps, the reported linkage of the Roman Catholic hierarchy with leading Nazis and Nazi escapes when they were defeated, the piles of skin-and-bone corpses of their victims bulldozed into pits.

LXIX."Stop! We also have among us despisers of roots. You were within one small hill of a nomad encampment when reaching your worst in the desert. You only just missed them, and they you."

LXX."Thank you telling me now."

LXXI.Her body collided with his, she scrambled astride him, pinioned his arms.

LXXII."You are grumbling again? It was lucky for

you and I that you did not know they were there, nor they you. Nomad hospitality is renowned and you might well have gone off them. You would not have been the first. Imagine. I would have listened to your coming to me and listened to your walking away from me. I may never have seen you."

LXXIII."You mean you would not have come after me?"

LXXIV.It stopped her. It was as if a clock had stopped ticking. "The poisonous trees," her voice was contained, "your interrogation's next angle, are there to keep out animals dangerous to us or our crops. If some among them ever make it among our crops, they will soon see to it that nothing is left to harvest."

LXXV."Why not just the fence?"

LXXVI."The core of the heatstorm of the red desert is central, a furnace-haven for the few, not unimportant, life-forms that have opted to live in such conditions. Their reasons are their own, and I am sure sound. More than a few creatures bypass the worse of the hotness, along less terrible ways, as you saw. Those ape creatures you encountered, and there are others, can rationalize and arrange, in a so-far limited way, and they must look at that desert and think "Not for me." But supposing they too took it into their heads to cross it, come this way. How would we stop them? Deter them? How would any fence? Forever. One day, the most formidable defence, the stoutest stone or metal, will decay. Sadly, all must die, and the poisons, of the trees and in the carcasses, do not hurt. The counsellors ensure it."

LXXVII."I heard groaning."

LXXVIII."Who and what does not groan on occasions? At least from frustration? On some days I must put up with you at it every two minutes. But think on it. They would be coming this way to eat us! After all, all humankind is on their time-honoured menu as little trouble to catch! Furthermore, leaning towards human attitudes, they could one day develop a further sobering ambition. They could be coming to conquer."

LXXIX.He failed to imagine being held up and munched like a banana.

LXXX.He heard her yawn long and hard, abandoning her prisoner.

LXXXI."Finish it, please, then I promise to shut up and be good. Atlantis now."

LXXXII."They fish. They trade anything they think can be traded. They bear arms from the day they can walk, in regiments based on their clan warrior societies. They are our perpetual nemesis. We can never know when they will come. Think on this, Ilex. We can never know. Not the people. Not you and I. We can never be sure, never know but must always be sure, always know. Dismiss all you know of what is meant by faith outside. Yours must be superior to the extremes. Do you understand me? Say you understand me!"

LXXXIII."I do but," his brain managed to pass it on to his mouth, he did not want to know but needed to "are you saying that war against us is trouble free for them until the tables miraculously turn? What has to happen before we make the opening shots, take the war to them first? Keep our wits peeled and hit them hard before they are ready?"

LXXXIV."With what?" she was sleepily puzzled.

LXXXV."With what do you think? A flock of field mice?"

LXXXVI."For the good health of our well-being here, all of us must endeavour to contribute to the well-being of all others wherever and whoever they may be. How would we by being aggressive? Marinating ourselves in bad quality would separate us from life's purest joys, to what gain? Our intentions must never be malignant or vengeful. Never. You may make war, fight in whatever is your way, and Machea, with your fighters or alone but the people, no! They must not."

LXXXVII.His hand clamped her mouth.

LXXXVIII."Hush. Tell me I am hearing things, then why we give a man a spear and call him a soldier? If they do not fight, what do they do?"

LXXXIX."Oh, they are not idle. Not every soldier is celebrating our wedding, lazing about, as you kindly put it. They are continually responsible for communications. We have secret shelters permanently manned. If trouble arises, they escort the people. They organize supplies. Atlanteans know of the shelters but not where they are, and rarely find out. Given no choice, the soldiers will resist, bodily defend, sacrifice themselves to gain time to give the people better opportunities of escape or try to draw the enemy soldiers away, make them waste time but never must they be the aggressors."

XC.She stretched, the emeralds drowsed. "I want sleep." She sank back, turned away.

XCI."It becomes dafter by the sentence."

XCII."Before you get worked up," she groaned crossly, "and dig into that large sack of sarcasm you always carry everywhere, let me challenge you to think of anything more manly that any man can do! You cannot! Do you think it child's play and painless for them? Because it is not. They have their own families to fear for."

XCIII."So why the spears etcetera?"

XCIV."To assist them, and they are the emblems of their pride."

XCV.His cheeks ballooned.

XCVI."Atlantis today? This night?"

XCVII."I do not know. We never know. I said that not one minute ago. It is not for us to know, or

123

interfere."

XCVIII."Interfere!" he gave a cracked laugh.

XCIX."Ilex," she yawned as if it were a final extended breath, "they are, they fish, they trade, they enjoy the perversions of Hadja."

C. "Do we not put our own people among them? Spies?"

CI. Silence.

CII.The images from the caves returned. That uplifted hand. A sickened sigh swelled his cheeks from a morbid sense of isolation and understanding of nothing, the faces of his father and mother urging him home, a distorted appearance of an unclear picture thinning. Gone.

CIII.His sudden chuckle made light of it.

CIV."Do you want me to build up the fire?"

CV."Not want anything." Her tongue was groggy. "Only sleep to remove me from you. You are the nosiest woman there ever was."

CVI."I thought men were the worst."

CVII."I was paying you a compliment."

CVIII.They slept, arms and legs entwined, covered only by the capacious star-adorned night.

CIX.He awoke with a start. To feet tiptoeing close, closer, close enough for him to see where brooding distortions quivered, peering down at him with dark luminous eyes. He huddled in frailness, clammy with sweat. A night bird sang a solemn hymn-song to the Death that had been with him ever since he had climbed into the plane, always waiting in patient certainty never far away, standing less than patiently over him now. He panicked not from terror of Death but terror of losing what lay beside him. The headiest wine. The supreme work of artistry. A spark streaked through a low arch of stars. A meteor deserting. As if at a signal, the distortions turned away, as a herd of deer walked away but not far and halting, turning towards him again, the spots of dark shine fixed upon him. Mistrustful. Memories and futurity in fusion. Mistrusting him. With good reason. He was inadequate.

CX."My love, my love," her palm cushioned his temple, "you are having a nightmare."

CXI."No. I am not trusted. Can you see them?"

CXII.She was at a rare loss. "I see them. But I think, far from having no confidence, they have brought their appreciative opinion of you by displaying their fellowship with you and how they can come and go and be as they please."

CXIII.Her soft fingers found him. Reading the demand she held in her hand, her knees folding outwards into the grass, her hand guided, she lay pinned to the grass through her groin. He gathered her buttocks, lifting her and her terrified whimpers emptied himself with blind tyranny into her screams, collapsing noises, dizziness. Small other movements fluttered on the edges, deer looking on as witnesses to an occasion. The night bird's hymn had ended.

CXIV.He cuddled her through a night of mental exhaustion.

CXV.

CXVI.They had knocked on the door minutes before and now they were drinking hot cherry juice in wooden cups in a log cabin in a garden of fruit trees and hives. It was the negroid man in his thirties of the house, Tampar, who had brought them the cherry juice and prepared and now brought them breakfast, baked apples sauced with hot honey, two each. Tora, the greying auburn wife, had taken their clothes in exchange for brown robes. She released the three children having passed her inspection, who scampered about with kisses all round, romped off to school. Both boys wanted to be animal doctors. The girl would inherit the trees and hives.

CXVII.Waving their appreciation to Tampar and Tora tending their fruit, the skies of rain pregnant clouds rumbled and dimmed as if towards early night. Hollows filled with shadowy mist. It disappointed him. He steered her under boughs to wait for the downpour to pass. Sitting against a knobbly trunk, spattered by drips, they ate cherries, drank more cherry juice. Not speaking. It was not always necessary to speak. Times came along when words would only get in the way. Nor did they have to say "I love you."

CXVIII.Rashida's toes made drawings in dead leaves. The first a horse's head, the next unrecognisable. He failed to work it out.

CXIX.But imagination rushed to attack him, a montage of bawling men, axes hewing contemptuous acts of butchery, shrill screams, death rattles, wailing children, two ghosts in yellow, his, hers, emerging from of their glass casket, ringed by bloodied, broken dead looking with hungry expectancy up at them. His lips tasted hers tasting of cherries, eclipsing of carnage and oppression of failure, recharging him, the skies turquoise, the land shiny. Her own hands bared her breasts with encouraging laughter. He knitted himself into the wild dream of her, her nails clawing deep into the small of his back. Deer looked on approvingly.

CXX.

CXXI.They bypassed camps of laughter. People knew of them but kept their distance. The variety of crops never ceased to astonish him. They called in at lonely homes. Sat with infants watching what frogs and fish were doing in a calm side pool of a mill stream, chatty among themselves and with the two unknown grown-ups.

CXXII.Thick yellow mist blotted out the dusk across the river. Drumbeats breathed in booming pulses. Two lights emerged following the far bank from their right, twin torches on an indeterminate mass forcibly parting the mist.

CXXIII. "What is it?"

CXXIV. "I do not know. It is certainly big, and may not be very nice but big and not nice does not have to be dangerous. The biggest lion in a pride can be its biggest coward."

CXXV. "Very re-assuring. There was a leopard that made friends with a fire," his arm wrapped her into protection. "Every day, the leopard went to visit the fire at his home but not once did the fire call on him. The leopard's mate teased him, and told him the fire was being a poor friend. The leopard went to see the fire again, and it annoyed his mate because the fire looked upon their home as being not worthy of a visit from him. The leopard begged the fire to come and visit them but the fire excused himself, saying he never called on anyone. The leopard pressed him hard, and the fire gave in but said he would need a road of dry leaves. The leopard told his mate. They strewed a path of leaves all the way from the fire's home to theirs. They tidied their home, and waited. They heard a strong wind and other noises outside. The leopards opened the door to see what it was. It was the fire at the door, and his fingers burned the leopards. The leopards ran back inside and escaped out of the window but their home was burned down, and leopards have been marked with burnt spots ever since, to remind them of the fire's visit. This Creator you talk about. How do you, we, believe it, he or she came about? Out of nothing?"

CXXVI. "Now?"

CXXVII. "The highest mountain of them all."

CXXVIII. "How that first, indiscernible disturbance of the non-existence was caused, who will ever say?

But, Ilex, even you cannot dispute that it did happen. That initial palpitation can only be described as a flicker of awakening, a spark of conscious energy to light the lamp of all and forever but imagine it then, reposeful in aware oblivion, for who can say how long, experiencing what must surely have been the most profound sense of peace but at some moment an ache, such as all living creatures possess but which humans alone can refuse to identify.

CXXIX.It was lonely.

CXXX.Picture it then, yearning for companionship with which to share the treasure of feelings. It summoned up and projected an image of itself, and lived on in sublime content with its twin until other sensations came to cause it concern. Unhappy that its twin too might be lonely, it conjured up a host of brethren, bringing into play all its profound visionary mastery, experimenting, fashioning from imaginative curiosity, judgement and portent every conceivable workable substantial and abstract prototype the primeval atoms could be made to concoct. On some, the Creator bestowed life as we know it, some as we do not, or furnished them with potential for life when the time was ripe, composed their necessities. He implanted them all with Himself as their vital underlying essence. Thus every disparate individual of every disparate genus and their disparate characteristics, abilities, functions and potential or not were made integral to the whole but all were left to decisions of fate.

CXXXI.You ask me: who and where is the Creator, how was He born out of nothing? That last I cannot say but his 'who and where' is the whole of existence, and non- existence. He is here with you and me, enfolding us and within us, and that monster too. All, yes you and I and that monster are part and parcel of Him, and He of us. To see him, you can look in your mirror. He is in your vanity. The Creator and the whole of existence, its every morsel, grain of dust, you and I, are the one."

CXXXII."So in your opinion, everything is nearly all spirit?" he could only put it that crudely.

CXXXIII.Without seeing it, he knew she smiled.

CXXXIV."Are you telling me it is not? Basing your reasoning on the fact that you cannot see it? When a blind man cannot see a whale, does that mean the whale is not there? When you admire yourself in your mirror, are you gazing at your thoughts? Have you ever once been able to spot that unphysical part of you which is you? No. It passes mildly through your mind as an abstract theory, yes, even now, after all you have been taught, and the effect of that is doubt, which is as silly as doubting yourself. When I say you are a king and god, how much of you will ever believe me? Then would you call me a liar? Am I? No. And yet you doubt, and your doubts will continue but no, my love, you are not in any way to blame.

CXXXV.The Creator's utmost longing is for a universal empire of many characters united as the one marvellous family by ability and zeal to attain the peace filled condition and creativity of Himself.

CXXXVI.Filled with that absolute promise with which his species is endowed, that lot fell upon this Earth's man.

CXXXVII.The Creator loves all His creations, yes, but man on this Earth and, I am sorry to say it, elsewhere, has caused Him regret. Furnished with potential to design their own fate, all the possibilities that lie within men have proved too much for all but a special few to bear. Filled with every impulse and sentiment, it is the weakness of man to follow the easy pathways marked by arrows of cheap satisfaction. Oh, men and women have their ties to what is best advisable and right but also many fallacies of vision, in particular the perennial conceit that their world and every star are made for their convenience and ego. Men and women would themselves be the Lords of the Creation and its every precious promise. Inwardly, they strain towards that original consummate potential but nonsensically, forgetful that they do not live long and lacking the will to accept the bug on the leaf as two indispensable ingredients of the whole. They are, and will come to know but will continue even then, digging their own graves and will not see stars again. How sad the Creator must be.

CXXXVIII.So, dearest, although it was not what you asked me, His home is in everything for He, or She, yes, is everything. As the body does not grow the head, nor does the Creator bring a baby to life but grows it as part of him but independent and granted that gift of person.

CXXXIX.He lives in all His works, sharing in His own exquisite artistry, and why not? He lives in every thistle's every thorn, every raindrop, each one of these breezes, every spider, moon and moonbeam, thought and feeling for all have the identical origin of being. He lives in the gods ordained by Him to be our guides and protectors for as long as our destiny will endure, which he has pledged need never end.

CXL.The fate of you and I has been to secure that pledge. More importantly, Ilex, your own pre-destination.

CXLI.You are my example. Distances exist between ideals, idealisms and practice, as you would prove for yourself when you set out on your flight. All your ideals were good and sound, and yet unsound because you would have become too enmeshed in trying to keep alive all your enterprise to have had time to unearth all those pasts or defend all those people across all that land, yet even as you were fighting your running battles with failure, you would have exerted extraordinary wilfulness to hold to every one of all your ideals. Because you are you. By that, you teach me to see sunny skies in my own troubles, and to understand how hard things must be and can become for our people for they are, after all, humans.

CXLII.One day we shall leave this Earth. Its human content is a burgeoning antithesis wrecking all balance catastrophically. It is so very wrong, and so suicidal, to eradicate the natural mix. Why do they not consider even their own children? Such diabolical irresponsibility.

CXLIII.So we will go. Our people. You and I. For myself, were I to go alone to the furthest reaches of the most distant galaxy, you would go with me, you would be there beside me. If I found myself in the most unyielding, darkest night, you would be with me as my personal sun. You are with me in my every activity, my personal spirit, my link with all else, although it has sorely distressed me and too many times when my eyes and my arms have not been able to claim you.

CXLIV.You take me beyond yet are part of the illusions. You keep me in touch with all the realities because you are my illusion who is my wondrously real, eternal beloved basking me in the sweet joys you bring me by being you.

CXLV.I feel your love when I make my many mistakes. When I am unfair to you, cross with you, lose my temper you never think to put me aside, no matter what else you may already be enduring because you, so imperfect, are my perfect one. You teach me to view from a less narrow point of view. Hourly, you are showered here with new, unlikely knowledge but it was I, so weary for so long from being without you, who have come close to losing the faith, dread that I had lost you such a cruel knife in my heart but now I have found you, you have given my faith back to me. Do not lose yours. Doubt, but do not surrender. Trust, as I trust you.

CXLVI.I do not feel alone any more, and will never again. Each and every step I take, wherever I will go, will be safe because you are with me, and I can put down my defences completely. I have only one desire for myself. You. When I was given you, the whole of Creation and more became mine. If storms blow, I have you to hold. My lantern that will never go out.

CXLVII.I am yours. You are mine. For the days remaining to us here, and throughout all that will lie beyond we will be together. My fears that I had lost you will not occur again. As the Creator is part of all things, I am part of you, and you of me. The vital part. For there is no me without you."

CXLVIII.His euphoria was total

CXLIX.

CL.Grey dawn greeted their awakening, drunk up by the rising sun. Noon of the tenth day found them at their honeymoon camp in their dell. The party-makers were no more but the fire had been laid. Rashida stripped on the stream bank, threw herself into the water splashing herself, rolling, washing herself more intimately. Carp swam about her close to the surface. He gave her space before he joined her. They sat on the bank for the air to dry them.

CLI.The day wore easily on. Day gave way to night. Night gave way to smoke coloured day.

CLII.Stars and moon gave way to day. Did not give way to sun.

CLIII.She took his hand, as something made him look over his shoulder. Deer were departing from the dell. In freedom and at peace.

CLIV.He knew he would not see them again. He too

was free. Of them. Of doubt. Free to be.

CLV. She took him home.

CLVI.

CLVII. "Ilex, Ilex! Quickly! Hurry!"

Her squeal cut across the width of the arena separating them and he was closing the gap before the last call was out, realising she was only looking into the dog pen. He trotted to her side. Her undiluted enjoyment paid him passing superficial attention.

"Five, Ilex. Five!"

"Oh, you fool."

She failed to hear. He sat on the wall. There was only Bruce to be seen, sitting underneath him and looking as woebegone as ever.

"Mata has thrown him out!"

The big hound heaved himself up.

"Bad luck," Ilex scratched the tawny scalp.

"Good for her," his wife enthused.

"How do you know?" he asked her cautiously.

It had all the hallmarks of one of her quirkier moods. He braced himself.

"Know what?" she demanded.

"Five."

"I looked."

"And now?"

"I am waiting."

"For?"

"For them to come out."

"You are in for quite a wait."

He had her full attention, uncomfortably. He studied her belly, there might have been a slight bulge or not. "When our baby is born, do you think he is going to be running about chasing a ball five minutes later? Any more than those pups are all set right now to come out and chase a few rabbits?"

"He?"

133

The emeralds arched in momentary consideration then confronted him with a beadier stare that reminded him of that big animal in the giant forest as they looked him up and down, equally unable to credit what they was seeing.

"He? What do you mean 'he'? You know it is going to be a boy? You are a magician suddenly?"

She flounced off, spun about, eyed him speculatively, came marching back, finger beating under his chin.

"And what do you mean 'our baby'? How do you know there is the one? What if I am carrying five, like Mata? Because you do not have a faintest idea of what is going on inside me, do you? And you will not be feeling full of magic when they are waking you night after night, all of them, for months after months because let me treat you to my guarantee that you are going to be helping me to feed them, wash them and change them!"

She stalked away, head high.

"Come along, idle!" he took it out on the dog. "Walk!"

By the time they returned, the prospect of quins had roused him, and he was more than a little hopeful.

Her efforts, and his, in her garden were re-doubled between quick walks outside.

Leaves were turning brown. There was no friendliness left in the lowering sky. Hurrying clouds tumbled. Winds hissed. Swaying trees clattered. Land appeared and disappeared among falling and rolling dead leaves.

They spent a day at their dell among rusted colours. A night of damp discomfort. Daybreak drizzled. Mid-morning rain burst like combers, last leaves flew.

The following morning, pale rags hung everywhere.

By noon, there was no day, no Earth.

CHAPTER NINE

Night-winter would endure for three months. Daily, astutely constructed tuition by mournful Semplar in the hieroglyphs unrolled a very visual language converting and conveying any and every topic into an explicit pictorial message, every mark and squiggle an unmistakeable component of a symbol that was its own unambiguous sketch.

Daily in his turn, Quita likewise took him under his sharp little wings to translate the Book Of Fate, episode by episode, which laid down the dwarf's two day discourse which apparently he delivered once a year. Artfully crafted with subtle variations, Quita repeatedly, guiltlessly, slipped into their conversations the role of the body as the soul's mortal carriage from which the soul alighted at death until the carriage drew up again. The illustration firmed, and by winter's end, Ilex had navigated through the Book of Fate from first word to last and finding none of it pretentious or unintelligible jargon. He resolved to make the return journey to the tunnel complex, itching to take a look at his camp, and the world beyond. Some of him was homesick?

"Skirting those ape things by miles."

"We both should hope it."

Of Settar he saw nothing, on the road the winter long as adviser, human and animal doctor.

Ilex applied himself to the lake, to a map and stills of the aerial cinematography, embedded it into his brain, an archipelago of thirty islands plus Hadja, an inhabited mud bank, detached fifty miles south, west of the lake inhospitable mountains, polar north, east a riot of tropical vegetation lacerated by water, at the

136

southernmost point, squeezing between mountains and tropics, the river a crooked finger poking in.

A small ensemble consisting of Rashida and male and female friends entertained with harp, marimba, lute and flute. She supervised the teaching of music and concerts, all ages joining in. Airs tuneful and jarring from medleys of instruments competed along passageways, Ilex delighted and intrigued when he came across a band of youngsters getting to grips with the erke, a wind instrument made of horn played by Bolivian peasants.

He exercised physically by working on the garden in the light of high flame torches like beacons, all crystal energy disabled, paralysed, swam religiously first thing and every evening. Reliant on flames for lighting, fires for cooking, the subterranean complex developed into a smoky rat hole of continuous suffocation, low ceilings, tight walls, people turning into blurred puppets, their hard edged voices gnawing his head until Rashida took him outside to a bullet-like snow-hail battering through the blackness and he was cured.

He had the spacious emptiness of the underside of the arena converted into a place of activities with vaulting horses, trampolines, high bars, balancing logs, pushing all youngsters and the gymnastics took enthusiastic wings. He introduced soccer, then a form of seven a side rugby which his father might not have recognized but which, amazingly considering their predisposition to non-violence, younger women as well as men took to, enjoying themselves not infrequently with mad frenzy, as if letting off powerful heads of steam.

***

137

Cushioned in the back of his Pontiac, a man was being driven into La Paz to purchase a birthday gift for his wife.

The Pontiac smoothly weaved its black and chrome passage past decaying shacks and their hustle and inertia of urban squalor that recalled the man's own base-born past.

"Stop!"

The Pontiac braked and slewed, the chauffeur convinced he had run somebody over although he had felt nothing, confirmed when he looked in his mirror. His boss was getting out. The chauffeur made a move of his own.

"Stay there."

The chauffeur was also the bodyguard. His hand found the Colt revolver under his jacket.

His boss was hurrying, calling out, towards a bunch of children, and a grubby little girl aged about seven walked to him worriedly, holding an inflated pig's bladder on a string.

They exchanged words, the man's smoothing, the street urchin abashed. Coins clinked into eager hands. Other hands dashed in at him, their palms too were filled and Morgan was on his way back to his limousine, staring at the bubble on its stick.

***

Winter ended. He lent a sweating hand on nearby farms going flat out, learning.

Came the Day Of The Sun, stung by the second sighting of their first incarnation in their caskets he cleaned the rifle, solicited Quita for lubricating grease, for ammunition to be made. When the dwarf baulked at that, he asked again forcibly without raising his voice.

"Quita, you will, repeat will, do it."

138

He made a note of the lights of satisfaction that appeared in the old man's eyes as he moved to comply. He thereupon requested Quita to make him a bow, short and double curved, with a range of at least fifty feet. The dwarf handed it over, made of wood combined with another material, with a batch of arrows the following day. He went to work on his archery. Rashida joined him on occasions, brightly half-hearted. As a way of honing eye-mind-hand coordination he made himself a leather sling, spent hours hurling stones; in an attempt to galvanize against complacency let it be known that he expected all men and youths to make bows and slings for themselves and practise. Practise! He told Quita to organize competitions. Unarmed combat, based on ju-jitsu, met with the foreseeable resistance until he declared it mandatory for every soldier to be proficient to a basic standard; took classes himself to produce a cadre of instructors, despatched them on tours of training instructors locally hand-picked. He recollected with embarrassment what that woman had done to him with a touch of her hand.

"Some are born able, some are not," Rashida informed him, adding the incongruity "you are not."

Something else that added up to not one iota of sense.

***

Morgan would not be dissuaded a second time, disregarding all reminders of the effects of weather, time and any scavenging birds. Money seduced, cut along wires and through red tape, arranged a balloon capable of lifting half a dozen men plus rescue gear in the States.

"Parachutists," an acquaintance in the French embassy suggested with Gallic flair.

"From the balloon?"

"Certainly. To secure it."

"Who would be brainless enough?"

His acquaintance could answer that too. Resident in Bolivia was a number of ex-foreign legionnaires, who very likely had parachuted in Indo-China, where many had jumped without being taught how. Some, he was cautioned, would doubtlessly be former SS stormtroopers.

"Irrelevant."

***

Within weeks, a granddaughter had been born to him, by the son whose corpse he had renewed his determination to retrieve.

They named her Maria Victoria; as the days went by, Rashida the driving force, Victoria stuck.

Inside Ilex, doubts and self-doubts were increasingly sporadic, losing ground to incredulity at his unsurpassable circumstance marred by lapses into longing to see the outside world again and anxiousness concerning his sanity, Settar's declaration of a "strong human strain" in his character underscored by the testimonies of Rashida that not all of him was human the most crackpot side to it all.

Bound up by her baby, shunning minders, Rashida put herself out to spend long hours with him, gave him long hours to be with himself.

Victoria's birth had blossomed her into another kind of woman, catering for the three of them with pleased efficiency.

"It is easy for me," she confided. "I know what I know. Know I possess all I could wish for. Being part of you, near to you, within sound of your footsteps is the only place I will freely choose to be, and through this little daughter who keeps holding your hand."

It was not for him to let her down, and peering long and hard frequently into the baby eyes a lighter green than her mother's, Victoria personalized and summarized absolutely and precisely the trust placed upon him, granted him, by these, his people. His.

It was not for him to fail them. Not a single one of them. Not a single baby. Born and not yet born.

Ever.

She took them off for rambles, Victoria strapped to his shoulders. Usually they took Bruce, and a pup from the litter Rashida had kept for herself, "Jupie", the reason never explained. Bruce had begun his decline, the solitary blot.

In a hamlet they came across the same band of erke playing children giving a concert, not the least embarrassed by being mostly out of tune.

He was at the mirror, considering his lack of need to shave.

"You conceited parrot!"

Next day, into his hand she pressed a small, pink framed looking glass painted with a pink parrot, patted his head.

"There. Preen your conceit at any time."

He familiarized himself with Venturia until only the lake, the far side of the river and the territory beyond the great wall held onto all their secrets.

Every trip ended with presents, stones that caught his eye, flowers; a baby tortoise for his daughter, which had her father not daring to come home the next time without one for her mother, even though she only had to ask virtually anyone, tortoises were common household pets.

His wife kept him high on his toes. There were days on end when he could only keep wondering what she

141

was going to be coming up with next. And he enjoyed every second.

Another sighting of his body in the glass casket was of his identical twin down to the bow. With it he was dextrous, Rashida almost a match, with the sling mediocre. The living Rashida was five months pregnant. Pregnancy, like motherhood, suited her. Though her stomach swelled grossly, they were carefully greedy when they wanted to be because they wanted to be.

"It is not my wish to upset you, Ilex, but do you know," she rested both hands on the lump, "it could be more than one this time."

He looked up from the box kite he was constructing. Kites were popular toys for young and old alike but he had not seen a box kite here and was already seeing the looks on faces.

"Why would it upset me? Do you not know how to find out for sure?"

"I do not wish to. I want it to be a surprise. But it could even be four, and if that is so, I will have to ask you to help me a very great deal, even in the middle of nights."

The green spotlamps closed and re-opened, centred on him.

"I look forward to it."

He went back to his kite, reduced once again to wondering if she was having him on.

Two weeks later, he made camp in the elmwood. Sat atop the great wall, viewing critically the secretive wild country, unreal, indistinct, the backdrop of mountains. The pathway vanishing into bushes directly below as if diving into hiding. Exhilaration prickled. The cause the unknown on offer below. There was nothing to see.

Nothing to hear. Wrong. Winds fussed audibly on both sides. Every breath drawing a response of leaf, twig, branch, each with its own peculiar note. Like a musician's fingers brushing strings. Playing many different sounds. Different voices. To creatures of the wild, quietness the element in which they felt best able to live in safety, sound was of vital significance. Sound was information, translated by trained ready ears. Every least rustle, wing beat, footfall. Snapping of a twig. The worm heard by the bird. Movement cleaved into his reverie. With an evasive whisper a deer broke cover onto the path, not twenty paces distant, glanced back at a querulous noise. An arching bound left only a fern frond nodding to a standstill.

He slept beneath the elms. Breakfasted on the wall on rye bread and apple juice. Readying his head. Gave himself no extra time. Dropped down. Opened the door. Held back, thrilling in alarm, ready to slam it shut again. Went through, shut it behind him, tested it to make sure, thoroughly aware that he was being dim-witted but urged on from within to see something, anything of where or what this path led to, padding cat-like, seething with feral instincts, hedged in on both sides by bushes, rueing not having the rifle. Bushes gave way to fig trees. From the feet of the figs, round eyed shaggy faces questioned this intruder. Another hung by its tail as it gawped. One of them whooped. The monkeys made their escape up the trees, clutching babies, followed him using hands, feet, tails, pausing when he faltered where the figs ended at a clearing, his darting eyes and brain taking stock of broken primitive stoneware, implements of bone and wood strewn where they had been thrown, a strong shack of logs, low, windowless, turf roofed, iron chimney pipe protruding, a lean-to shed over a woodpile. A locking bar swivelled. He peeped into stale darkness, uncovered a single room, tools and pots on shelving, an iron stove, piled sticks, raised wooden boards for a bed. Behind the shack, dark rich soil had once been tilled, corn now running wild losing out to ferns and crushing feet. A warning rang in his head. Did not deter his feet. A dip was to a stream running between ferny banks, criss-crossed by markings. Ferns shook, clattered, startled him, ducks quacked in take-off under his feet, left him breathless. He splashed his face, drank, the water refreshing, his heart uncomfortably fast. He sighted vultures circling, stark reminders of how much this was a bad place to be. The path crossed the stream into a forest of palms and rank undergrowth. Groans stopped him, enveloped in sweating nervousness. The air was still but the forest sounded and felt under torture. Trunks were hideous with knobs and outgrowths. He waited on high alert, racked by the urge to turn and run, desperate to see what he could not see, with a determination he was unable to resist trod with jumpy caution between ugly groaning trunks. Crows squabbling on a putrefying heap took to the air squawking irritably at being disturbed. By him? He waited, enforcing sweating control. The path widened enough to take a lorry, pitted. Enough flies rose from splatterings of dung to feed an army of birds. The air took on a peppery savour. Bamboo crowded brokenly, strewn with chewed bits. Records of what? Leafy movement whirled him about. Feet brushing softly. Instant instinct sent a prayer to somewhere. He stalked on, breathing hard, eyes, ears, the whole of him straining ahead, side to side, piercing overhead leaves, swivelling repeatedly to check what was behind, the bamboo athrob, stealthy cracklings hammered his pulse in his temple. The air tasting sugary. Blue reeds with blue flowers fringed a broad water hole, a buffalo drinking knee-deep. It shook its horns with whistling snorts as wide eyed and wide eared he picked his bouquet, put them carefully into his pack. If he could get them into water once a day they might keep.

A bamboo alley sucked him along it, straight as a spear, dropping...he stopped, grimly excited, absorbing the grey back in the trench just below him. An elephant. In a pit dug by people? Its end on the stakes must have been excruciating. But they would surely have come running when they heard it screaming...the head moved, the ears flapped, there was no urgency...

Where was the herd? He must have just come through it. He took a deep anxious breath, went down. Vultures in a sweep of sky looked as if they all had their eyes only on him. The ears ceased flapping. The head did not move but the eyes found him sideways. The trunk curled to sniff him. It was a small elephant, looked less than half grown, the backbone level with the lip of the trap or subsidence. The ears flapped leisurely as he pulled out his knife. For what felt like the rest of the day he cut and scraped a shelf, straining to not lose focus on every inch of his surroundings, probed by the trunk missing out no part of him but at last it was done and he retreated back up the slope and out of the way.

The elephant did not move, though it could have done and the shelf looked right but it only lifted its trunk. He went and stood behind it, poked its rear end with his foot. The elephant squeaked. Clambered out. Sawing-gabbling puffs from somewhere snapped the last of his nerves, turned him towards too far away safety barely reining in the impulse to sprint. Warmth touched his neck, the elephant's trunk, hurried him on, the elephant keeping up, outstretched trunk feeling. A puffing siren spun him, brain and strength numbed by the green bipedal head crowded with knives pacing along the alley leaving showering bamboo in its wake.

It came to a stand. A petrifying image, red eyes restless, revolving, lips writhing, boasting their fangs. He held himself rigid but shivering. It had not seen him or the elephant. The elephant flapped its ears. The red eyes pounced. The green legs churned and he entered the headlong, terminal race for his life, bamboo scraping his face, the elephant breathing into his neck, a puffing stamping overhauling. Bamboo splintered in destructive action. A peal of trumpeting thunder. A grey monster burst over him, missed him with a thud, he hurled himself at leaves hanging low, scrambled upwards, remembrance flooded with the dinosaur's size and reach, climbing, climbing, cowering into leaves, below him a giant tusker butting, goring, trampling a green bulk, a much smaller elephant looking on. The great bull charged once more, with lethal fury impaled with its tusks the green body once more. With a trumpeting scream of final tantrum, shaking its head, trunk waggling with the motion, it stared down at the fruits of its destruction, escorted the young elephant away.

What had to be the last great hunting dinosaur on Earth lay dead on the ground but Ilex remained shakily buried on his safe perch in the crown of the palm.

Somewhere in his head ruminated blearily. Should he organize some men to fetch the bones to put them on display?

A brown block browsed itself mouthful by mouthful into the scene and alongside the dead giant. The buffalo must have grown used to the fact of the dead.

The dead snout lifted. The buffalo wheeled about, wheeled again. The dinosaur struggled upright, churned into full limping pursuit.

Setting course for home in the straightest line he could remember, the biggest wild animal he saw was a hare.

Rashida was speaking with some women in the arena. He held out his blue reeds, more dead than alive but they looked as if they could be revived.

The emeralds spat them aside, her face flushed and darkened. The finger lifted.

"What have you been doing? Where have you been doing it? No, I do not wish to hear! And especially a lie!" Finger and copper-crimson face raged at him. "Do you think I do not know the only place where these can grow? You grow, Ilex! Grow up! Like that man who was your father said to you until he wearied of it. Grow up, Ilex! Grow up!"

***

The farmhouse and every barn were a gaudy yellow.

Setting out at first light, he set about sowing a strip of six acres with flax, back and forth, back and forth, back and forth. A box strapped to his chest contained the seed, spilling down into a dish spinning rapidly to a pulley in his right hand and strewing the seed. The day before, by himself behind a horse he had ploughed, rolled, harrowed and rolled again the six acres to make a level seed bed, wearily patted himself at the end on the back. Fragments of conversation drifted from other fields where others were at work. It was gone noon when a small girl came to fetch him. He returned to the yellow farm for a break.

He found Rashida on all fours in a patch of garden freshly turned over, the fork nearby, humming to herself, planting potatoes from a basket, concentrating to achieve straight rows. She joined him on a bench nailed to an outside table, eyes shining, a redness like fires on her cheeks.

Flower smells tempered farm smells. On a stretch of lawn, in the middle of the pack, being knocked about and trampled underfoot, Victoria was yelling her head off, caked in mud and grass. The shade of red roses hanging in showers held the white crib of James.

"She likes nothing better than being a mess," Ilex asserted.

It was a walled garden splendid with flowers, his wife one of them, the emeralds an incandescence displaying the unfettered well-being with which she felt endowed.

"She does but she is a lamb."

Calls of livestock, the children at play, clockwork squeaking of the vanes of an old wind pump turning jerkily at the top of its wooden tower were mellow echoes floating through lazy air. A light wind shepherded clouds. In a side yard adjacent to the house where their waggon was parked, a little fat half-naked Caucasian woman examined their horses' feet. In a nearby field, a man and youth were pitching hay.

They poured damson juice out of a porcelain jug into porcelain beakers.

"How can they be getting on? I am dying to know."

She looked along the sub-valley in the direction of where Settar and Quita would be, at a neighbouring farmstead dealing with a calf born with two heads. It was the chit-chat topic of the day. Ilex was more than curious as to how it would cope if it had to be left with both heads.

She chuckled at a flock of bantams led by a colourful cockerel pelmet after a dragonfly.

"There are folk outside who accuse dragonflies of sewing your eyelids together while you are asleep," he let her know.

"Dragonflies must know some good stories. They were here long before tortoises and those dinosaurs."

A giant tortoise trundled by.

It was the usual menagerie. Eland grazed an

extensive paddock. A venerable mule swished its tail at the flies, tethered to a maple alongside an old wolf. They had been foal and cub together. A water buffalo's doleful head loomed over a gate, its hooves in a dam-raised waterway, where two cormorants spread their wings on a moored raft. The tortoise added mildly to the melee of children by altering course towards them. They scampered off, leaving the tortoise plodding doggedly on towards nowhere.

To add to it all, it was a family of ten from a positively pretty, red headed teenage girl to a boy of Victoria's age, one of the ragamuffins in the same mess as she.

Hala, the sagging ball of white blubber dealing with the horses, was famed for her artistry with cloth. She had presented Rashida with a saffron gown, homespun from her own silkworms. The eldest daughter in a fetching orange dress and veil squatted on a blanket in the shade of a damson tree with a roll of red satin, out to emulate her mother.

"Fishing later, Ilex?"

"Why not?"

Kolar and his son had come in from the hayfield. Kolar was a dark bearded bear of a man, the effortless attempts to rid himself of the last of the hay suggesting loudly a reservoir of brawn untappable by any amount of hard labour. Snubbing the damson juice, he helped himself to a beaker of honey wine from a pitcher, homemade thanks to his bees and a lavender field which also yielded medicines, oils for perfumes and for Kolar's unlikely hobby of decorating the porcelain he made. Another enterprise was ownership of the two cormorants he fished his dam with. He had raised them under a hen.

"They thought I was a murderer when I popped them in the water."

149

If he had a pride and joy, it was his troop of golden tamarinds under the strict thumb of the head female.

Kolar swallowed his wine, observing with good humour his son's heavy footed traipse into the house poured himself another. A man who did few things by halves.

"Leather tomorrow, Ilex. Perhaps you can lend me a hand."

In baths in a shed set aside, Kolar tanned leather on his own behalf and for the wider community, by placing layers of bark, leaves and fruit over hides and adding water impregnated with salt."

A daughter of perhaps twelve arrived with a tray of hot cakes baked by her. The pack caught the whiff, scampered in, seizing fistfuls of cake threw themselves in a munching bunch on the grass. Victoria did her best but came a long way last. Ilex fed her pieces of cake on his lap. Her face turned bright red as she choked and coughed crumbs and currants out. Shooting him a glance of not amused exasperation, Rashida took daughter and all the cake from him. With the children concentrating now on fast eating, another voice was raised, that of Hala, now coming from a hen house with a basket of eggs and demanding Kolar, something to do with the state of the hen house. To father ten was rare but Kolar's industry kept them well provided. His little fat wife seemed strict with him, in spite of barely reaching his chest but Ilex surmised that Kolar did not do badly. Looking suitably chastened, Kolar ambled off to the house for his wash.

First famishments eased, mouths still stuffing with cake produced a rumpus of requests for stories from the world he had come from; springing him into the once and for all decision to get his self-promised trek back to the tunnels underway, and take volunteers with him, and all of them would explore it all. The volunteers could act as guides thereafter for interested parties.

"SPLISH-SPLASH!" He hooted with laughter as his bellow seized young startled attention. "If all the seas were one sea, what a big sea it would be. If all the trees were one tree, what a big tree that would be. If all the axes were one axe, what a big axe it would be. If all the men were one man, what a big man he would be and if that big man took that big axe and chopped down that big tree and it fell into that big sea, what a big splash it would be!"

Young blank faces left him feeling inane. He could not bring himself to look at the emeralds.

"Midas," he tried again, "was a king who did a service for a god of wine called Bacchus, and the god permitted him to choose whatever reward he pleased. So King Midas asked for everything he touched to be turned into gold, and his wish was granted. The food he ate, the clothes he wore, the water he drank and bathed in, the very sands he stepped on after bathing, turned into gold, and soon he had no comforts at all in his life, nothing to eat and drink. He then made matters worse by giving his opinion that Pan, a god of rural people, made better music than Apollo, who was a prince among the gods and also the god of music. Apollo got his own back by giving Midas ass's ears."

He could not remember how it all ended for Midas but it seemed to have gone down better.

"A girl found a shell on a river bank. She placed it on a rock while she looked for more. She did not find any more, and then forgot all about the shell on the rock until she was home. She asked her friends to go back with her but they said no, it was nearly night time and dangerous animals would soon be about. The little girl had to go alone, and she sang to keep up her courage. On the rock sat an elf. He asked her to sing again, and as she sang he captured her and imprisoned her in a barrel. He went from village to village with his barrel, offering to play good music in exchange for meals. When the elf beat his barrel on the outside, the girl sang on the inside and the people gave the elf lots of food. The elf became famous. He reached the girl's own village. The people had heard of him and asked him to play. When the girl sang, her family recognized her voice and they gave the elf lots of wine to make him fall asleep. They rescued the girl, and put wasps in the barrel, and made a small hole in it. The elf did not know, and the nest time he beat the barrel he was badly stung."

The young faces were not entirely blank. One little girl's lips quivered.

He puffed out his cheeks.

"A baby seal did not want to swim. He was lazy and badly behaved. His father carried him out into the sea but as soon as his father let go of him, the baby seal swam back to the beach because he did not like water. On the beach, he lay in the sunshine with his fat little stomach pressed against a nice warm rock, and slept. His mother shuffled closely behind him, put her nose to his back and gave him a big push, and the little seal flew through the air and splash! Into the water he went! He tried to get out, shouting to his mother all the bad things he thought of her. She pushed him back in again, and when he tried to get out again she whacked him hard with her flipper. He tried to get out again. She pushed him under. He swam away until he came to another part of the beach, where he crawled out onto the sand, cross and sulking. Soon he fell asleep. The sand became hot. The sun became hot. Everything became too hot for him but the little seal felt too lazy to move to the cool water, and he did not like water anyway, so he lay and suffered and sulked, until small waves of water crept out of the sea and over him. The feeling on his skin was very enjoyable, and before long he was playing half in the water, half out, rolling about and practising his swimming strokes without realizing it. When the tide covered the beach in deep water, there was the baby seal playing up and down through the waves. He decided he liked swimming, and swam off to join some other baby seals, and they all played together and tried to catch a fish but the fish laughed at them and dodged them easily, but after that the naughty baby seal was always in the water.

"One day, a large fin broke the surface close to where the young seals were playing. Father seal was on the beach. He saw the fin and barked. It was a shark. The baby seals swam to the shore, all except the naughty one. He heard his father's bark and saw his playmates swimming away as fast as they could but he carried on playing. He had never liked doing as he was told. Why should he now? He hung upside down in the sea until his lungs were ready to burst. When he looked again, he was all on his own; his playmates were all on the beach. He heard more anxious barks but started playing again, and all the time the fin was coming closer and closer. The naughty baby seal did not know. He did a somersault, dived deep then swam up and jumped out of the water, just as a row of teeth flashed underneath him. The shark's rough body scraped him, the tail struck him hard, spun him over and over. He saw a great mouth and great teeth but he was helpless, spinning round and round and very, very frightened. He tried to swim to the shore. His baby flippers worked hard. He saw his mother swimming towards him. She was frightened too, she knew about sharks but her baby was precious to her, no matter that he was naughty. She knew that a shark attacked from underneath. She saw the fin disappear close behind her baby. She knew the shark was about to attack him. She dived and swam as fast as she could beneath the little body of her baby, her eyes on the shark. The shark turned over and aimed its teeth up at the tired little seal. Its jaws opened wide. The mother seal rammed it, bit it. The jaws snapped shut but missed her baby. The shark was surprised by the unexpected thing that had happened to it and swam out to sea but turned to attack again. It was hungry. But the mother seal pushed her baby through rocks where the big shark could not follow and into shallow water. She had saved her baby, and the naughty little seal was never naughty again."

He had them in the palm of his hand. He told them the story of Noah and the flood and his ark and all the animals.

"What did they all eat?" a small boy earnestly demanded to know.

A wail from the roses saved him.

He received his daughter back into his care. His eyes went with Rashida. She had put on weight since the birth of James but it detracted nothing from her, if anything added to her.

She seated herself beside him again, the white bundle busily feeding. It set him off on attitudes to breast feeding in public outside.

"For some, the idea is genuinely repugnant, and for some it is illegal."

"They must believe nature itself is repugnant," Hala relieved him of Victoria, sat on the grass.

"According to religious scriptures, women exposing themselves drive men to lust. In certain societies, women are not allowed to show so much as even their eyes outside their homes."

"Advice like that is back to front," Kolar went to sit with Hala with a beaker full and the pitcher.

"The scriptures themselves are not always to blame," said Hala. "The founder of Mohammedanism

154

described extremists as entering the faith on one side and coming out the other like an arrow through a body. He was correct, to my mind. You learnt that story of the seal when you were a boy, Ilex?"

"He did not need to learn it," Rashida wiped the baby's mouth. "The naughty little seal was named Ilex. For shark, you can read any and every unintelligent risk you can think of."

"We did hear you are well disposed towards elephants," Kolar's shoulders shook to his beefy chuckle.

Ilex brushed it aside, turned to Queen Victoria's likening of babies with cabbages.

"Your cormorants are the same as last year?"

"The same. Good birds. I had to my work cut out convincing them that they were not hens."

"You two met through a hen," Rashida joined in.

"Oh yes," Hala bubbled. "He had been sent out to look for a pullet. You thought a wildcat had taken it, didn't you? You caught a wild woman instead."

"You both turned out to be good layers." Kolar dodged a swipe at his ear. "I saw it in a yard and ran in. A door opened and she scared me stiff. I was fifteen and shy, and all set to run for cover but she chattered away and I stayed. She was only twelve but what a talker! I keep asking her to teach the parrots, then I can be like the elf with my touring parrot choir. But I think it would be no bad idea," he mused, "to domesticate elephants more than we do." A sudden laugh convulsed him. "Bulls are blessed with good fortune. A bull and a cow are fine together until she is conscious of her calf soon to be born. From then on, she is pre-occupied with it. The bull gets the message and leaves. The cow links up with other females, and when her time comes they stand by her to guard her and sometimes even help deliver the calf, and woe betide anything which comes near that calf. They help bring it up. The bull is left to his own devices. To my mind, he has it made. That lad has it made."

"Slow down on that wine. What more silly things do their scriptures have to say about nature?" Hala asked.

"I can only really quote from the book of the Christians, which tells them their god has given them dominion over all the fish in the seas, all the birds in the air and all the beasts in the fields, and they accept that literally. Everything everywhere is theirs to do with however they like. Christians are not alone. Economics globally make a mockery of any thoughts given to tomorrow. There is no such thing as preservation. A decade or so ago, a war spread all over the globe for five years. After it, the seas gave bumper harvests because the fish had been pretty much left alone because of threats to fishing boats from enemy ships but ever since the peace the fish have been netted as if there literally is no tomorrow and by now the fish stocks must be well run down, and there cannot be long to wait before there are no fish left to catch. They must see it coming but they do not seem to care."

"Who could hope to be sustained by their kind of economics for long?" came the unassuming deliberation from Hala. "And they clearly do not care about any who are wholly reliant on fish, humans and others. Nor, astonishingly, do they even seem to have any regard for themselves. With sensible management, as that war must have proven, the fish could return and remain and provide. But what is happening is not so abnormal. When you think of it, cycles characterize most things, long term and short. Plenty becomes scarcity. Today a sea, tomorrow a desert. Today I am rich, tomorrow I need help."

Ilex digested it. He said:

"People who receive help do not always clap their

hands for long. For centuries, Russia was a cruel, cruel country if you were only a serf. Landowners used to gamble their serfs. Losers in a game of chance would give servants away to the winner, usually women, of course, dragged out of their homes but some ninety years ago, an emperor, Alexander, put an end to serfdom, and forty million Russian serfs were set free. They became a kind of free peasant. They were given education, and other radical reforms were in the pipeline. Their liberation had cost the emperor six years of arguments with his nobility, who owned all the land between them. The good times for the liberated peasantry were cut short. They were allowed small farms but could only purchase land from the nobility, who pushed the price of land sky-high, or they were sold infertile land which could not grow enough to feed their families but they were still obliged to earn sufficient income from that land to meet the payments for it. One bad harvest, one sick cow left them worse off than ever before. Emperor Alexander had been hailed 'the liberator' but liberation turned into festering grievance. He was walking in a park with his family, accepting the cheers of a crowd. A man attempted to shoot him. The bullet missed but the new-found freedoms went into sharp reverse. Suspected threats to social order were exiled to labour camps in Siberia, a remote, empty region frozen for half the year where Russia traditionally sends its unwanted. Alexander had not lost his concern for the poor, and he was in his carriage with a document containing a new constitutional package that would allow the people to elect representatives who would help make up the laws. A bomb went off under the horses. Alexander was unharmed, and he was trying to help some who had been injured when another bomb exploded, and for him that was that. Thank you and goodnight. The nobility of

Russia are gone. Russia is now a strictly socialist state. The state owns and runs everything, supposedly on behalf of the people. Russia is still a cruel, cruel place. Half the world is dominated by more or less the same socialist system, half by market forces. Churches hover like vultures. If a desert can be made out of good grass, no matter how badly those who rely on it suffer, you can expect it to happen if it can make somebody richer, socialist, marketeer or servant of a god, with not many exceptions."

"Richer!" barked Kolar. "What is richer? Throttling your cockerel when you want it to crow?"

Ilex opened his mouth.

Whatever the words, they would never be formed.

From somewhere came a thumping of feet. A soldier kicked open the gate, sweat and dust lathered. Rashida emitted a small cry.

With a flick of a hand, Ilex went unwillingly to meet him, crushing a paroxysm of fear.

Pushing the man into shade was child's play. He waited for the heaving lungs to subside.

Dully, he saw the soldier's hand wipe at the dried lips, the bloodshot eyes that found him.

The breathing steadied. The dried lips moved. A cracked voice tolled in tumbling darkness.

"Ilex. The men from the lake. They have come."